Trading Poisons

Angel Lepire

Produced by:

FriesenPress
Suite 300 – 852 Fort Street
Victoria, BC, Canada V8W 1H8

www.friesenpress.com

Distributed to the trade by The Ingram Book Company

Dedication

FOR ALL THE STRONG WOMEN in my life, especially my mother and my sister. Thank you for teaching me, not just to overcome adversity, but to knock it down and take its shoes.

Acknowledgements

THIS BOOK WAS SUPPORTED BY the work of many. My life is supported by many more.

Thank you to my incredible editors; Leah Siewert, Robin Hawkins, Hannah Engle, and Sue Callahan. I, and all reader who successfully made it though junior high English, sincerely appreciate it. Speaking of junior high English, thank you to Kay Barker, and all teachers who encouraged me and other kids to pursue what they enjoy. If you ever wonder if you made a difference in someone's life…yes, you did.

Thanks to Joey, who will always be the only other person who understands why I turned out the way I did. My parents, siblings, in-laws, and for the rest of my family, who have always supported me through successes and screw ups. Whether it is by marriage, unending friendship, or you just got the short end of the biological stick, thank you for always being my "peeps." I love you all.

To my babies, who are the best three things I ever did. You will always be my soul.

This book would have truly never been finished without two people. Thank you to Rene, who helped me many days with kids when I was tired from writing all night, gave me the room to work when I needed it, and taught me the true meaning of unconditional love. Lynette, were it not for your support, encouragement, compliments, kind words, and (wonderfully charming) nagging, this would still be 30 pages in a Word document instead of an actual novel. Thank you does not begin to cover my appreciation for always believing in me, especially when I didn't. Love, love, love you both for all that you've helped me to achieve! Thank you.

God, thank you for the experience of this incredible life.

One

IT'S REALLY A PRETTY LONG *drive,* Jorie thought to herself. *Probably too far to drive alone.* She took a drink of the flavored water in the bottle on the small wire table, then a long drag of the cigarette she held in the same hand. As she watched the smoke float up into the dusk air, she wondered who she could get to go with her on the trip. *Rhea's most likely the only one who would do it,* she considered. Saddened by the fact that the list of people willing to help her had become so pathetically short, she nodded to herself that the decision was final. There were few others in the world she would want with her on this trek anyway. Rhea was the right person to ask.

Jorie made the phone call and set the plans in motion. Rhea was, as always, gracious and happy to help. It occurred to Jorie that as her years under Rhea's sponsorship passed, she had come to rely on the funny, wonderful woman in more ways that she could count. She woke up each day wondering if this was going to be the day Rhea would say she was done. That Jorie was too much; too much work, too much worry, too much hassle. That day had not yet come, and she was cautiously optimistic it never would. Even so, it seemed wise not to push her luck. In that sense, Jorie tried not to ask more of Rhea than was reasonable for a sponsor. The line of reason sometimes came at different points for the two women, and Jorie was always grateful when Rhea would kindly but firmly reestablish the boundaries rather than send her packing. There were not many like her in the world. At least not in Jorie's life. Not anymore.

The days that elapsed seemed to drag when Jorie was hoping for them to speed by, and to fly when she was wishing the clock would stop. So many feelings bounced inside her she barely knew which ones to pay attention to first. Mostly though, it was that longing to get it over with that dominated her days. It was as if there was nothing she could concentrate on until it was done.

The morning of the trip, Jorie sat on her front step at least an hour before Rhea was due to pick her up. She knew she would have only gas stops every few hours for smoke breaks, and thought she better get all her nicotine in while she had the chance. Actually she wasn't smoking half the cigarettes she lit. She would light one, hold it, watch it, take a couple of drags and put it out. This went on until Rhea pulled up in front of Jorie's rental. Rhea shook her head as she got out of the driver's side and pulled up the back hatch.

"Enjoying that cancer stick, are you?" Rhea asked, smiling.

"Quite, thank you," Jorie answered back with a nod. As she got up and grabbed her suitcase in her free hand she looked at the smoking stick held between her fingers. "You're not really suggesting I give up something else right now, are you?"

Rhea shook her head and helped Jorie get her bag in the back of the car. "Not at all. Just spray on some of that flowery perfume stuff you have. I don't care for it or the cigarette smell, but together they're somehow bearable."

Jorie chuckled as she dug through her purse for the body spray Rhea had referred to. She could still be surprised at the woman's eccentricities from time to time. This 'perfume and smoke' was a new one.

"Got your passport?" Rhea asked.

Jorie held up the small blue book without a word, and tapped it on the frame of the car door as she climbed in the passenger seat.

On the floor she placed the small wooden box.

The two women were quiet as they headed down the road. For Jorie, this was a dangerous place to be. She tried to force her attention on the buildings that swept past the car windows, the manicured lawns of the homes, the bright flowering hedges separating the lanes of the highway. Anything to keep her mind in the present, but the draw of her memories was strong. She gave into them, and her mind floated away.

A man's hand ran across the small of her bare back. As she reached her arms over her head, he gently pulled her shirt up past the long scars that lined them. He held her shirt for a moment against her body before throwing it on the floor behind her. His blue eyes opened for a minute as their lips parted, and Jorie felt as if he were looking past her soul. She brought her thin fingers up to his face. His rough face that had needed a shave that day, though there wasn't time. She let her hands fall to his chest and wound them through the mass of hairs there. Her breath was shallow she dropped them again to the button of his jeans. Jorie felt sick, partly because of the intense passion that was overtaking her, and partly because this man was not her husband.

She forced herself back with a jolt, kicked her flip-flops off onto the floor of the car. She pulled her legs up on the seat, resting her chin on her knees. This was a physical feat she would never have been able to even consider just a few years earlier. That thought jerked her back to another warm summer day, in what she called her "old life," that may have truly been the beginning of the journey she was now on. Feeling there was no further down she could possibly fall, it occurred to Jorie that this might be what was meant for her, right then, at that time. Maybe in her head was exactly where she needed to be right now. Rhea seemed to sense it too, and was happy to drive along in silence, allowing Jorie time with her own thoughts.

Though it now seemed a lifetime ago, Jorie could clearly remember the day just four years earlier that had changed everything in her world. She didn't know why that particular day stuck in her head as a turning point. It was really no different than a thousand other days in her seemingly ordinary life. Maybe it was because it was when Ryan mentioned the tree. That was probably it. She had been over it and over it in her mind, trying to decipher exactly when it could have been, and all she ever came back to was the tree. They needed somebody to help get rid of that damn dead tree.

Two

THE SUN FELT BLISTERING THROUGH the glass of her minivan as she pulled up in front of the large house. She grabbed her bag from the front seat and went in through the garage door. The instant she walked into the house she heard shouts coming from the basement.

"Give that back!"

"No way. It's mine. Who said you could play with it anyway?"

Jorie poked her head around the corner in the basement play room and smiled slightly. Even when they fought, her boys were the lights of her life. She wanted to be stern with them, but often felt it might break their spirits. She put a hand up and approached the two boys fighting on the floor over a train.

"What's the chance that I could make that train mine?" Jorie asked, crossing the floor to where they sat. She longed to sit down with them, play with them, just for a few minutes. But she knew it would be too hard to get on the floor. And nearly impossible to get back up again.

Brennan looked up at his mother with pleading eyes. "Mom, I had that train first, and Jack took it away. I was playing with it." He seemed somewhat relieved that the cavalry had arrived to rescue him from being bullied by his older brother.

"Jack, did your brother have that train first?"

"But mom, it's MINE..." Jack began, holding the train behind his back out of the younger boy's reach.

"Jack, we share our toys in this house. If he had it first, let him play with it, or you could play with him. There are lots of trains." Jorie felt as though she made this same speech every day. It didn't seem to take. Jack opened his mouth to make another objection, but the look on his mother's face told him it would be better to do as he was told. He reluctantly tossed the train at Brennan's leg, got up and stormed off in a huff.

Brennan, with the same beseeching look on his face, gave his mother a grateful smile. "Will you play trains with me mommy?" he asked.

"I would love to Bren, but I have groceries to put away." At least it was an honest excuse.

His head fell, and he quietly whispered, "OK."

The sound of a lawn mower hit Jorie's ears, and she turned her head to look out the basement window. She saw her husband Ryan walk by and then move out of view. She smiled back down at Brennan, and tousled his hair.

"You'll see, Jack will be back to play when he's done pouting."

Jorie went back upstairs and checked the video monitor in the kitchen. She saw her baby girl asleep, her arms over her head in what they liked to call her stick-em-up position. Jack was sitting on the couch, aiming a remote at the large flat-panel TV hanging on the back wall. Jorie considered sitting to talk with him, but she needed to get her groceries put away. There wasn't much time to get supper on the table before the baby would be up from her nap.

As Jorie unpacked food from plastic bags, she opened a box of granola treats and dug into a small package of the chocolate flavored gems. Before all the items were put away, Jorie had burned through three more packages of the granola treats. She knew the word granola didn't make them healthy, but she only really worried about "health foods" when she was on a diet, which wasn't this week.

"Hey babe," came her husband's voice from the garage door. Jorie barely glanced up from counter where she was chopping onions to put over the pot roast. "Do you have anything else to bring in?"

Jorie shook her head. "I got it all, but thanks. Done mowing?"

"Yeah, but we should probably have somebody over to look at that dead tree in the front yard. It's going to have to come down sooner or later." Ryan washed his hands in the kitchen sink, and kissed her on the cheek as he dried them on a towel. "That looks great."

"I'm just trying to get it in the oven before the baby wakes up," Jorie said as she nibbled on a slice of deli cheese. She finished preparing the meal, and then put it in the oven just as Grace's crying filtered through the monitor.

Jorie was about to go up the staircase when the pictures lining the wall caught her eye. She stopped and looked a wedding picture of herself; Ryan and the rest of their wedding party standing in front of several willow trees. She was not thin, but definitely smaller than after having three kids. There were also pictures of Ryan as a child, Jorie at her college graduation, and two large black and white pictures of her great-grandparents. Neither of them wore smiles, and appeared to look right through the camera lens.

Jorie straightened the frame holding a picture of her family shortly before her parents divorced. She and her sister Addie had always hated that picture, but it was one of the few taken of the four of them together as a family. Her chest tightened a bit. It always did when she thought about her family. She often wondered what her mom and dad would be like as grandparents. If her sister would have had kids...

Grace's cries became more insistent. Once she was up, Jorie checked on the boys, who had forgotten their earlier squabble and gone back to playing together. She set the baby in her high chair, and took out a box of Cheerios from the cupboard. Jorie put a handful on Grace's tray, then took another handful and threw her head back to make sure she didn't drop any on the floor as she ate some herself.

The rest of the evening went on as usual. They ate dinner together, though it was in front of the T.V. in the family room. Ryan had the remote of course. He flipped between the news and a history show about the Civil War. The channel surfing drove Jorie crazy, but she wasn't paying too much attention. There was a German chocolate cake cooling in the kitchen, and that was mostly what was on her mind. She was also making mental lists of all the things she needed to get done around the house the next day, what to send with Jack for the food drive at school, and how to get out of a jewelry party she had no interest in attending. And hadn't Ryan said something about needing to get rid of that old tree in front of the house? She decided to leave that one on his honey-do list.

The next Saturday afternoon Jorie had just finished the macaroni and cheese the kids didn't eat. The trash can was full, mostly of wrappers from things she had eaten the night before when she was sitting on the computer playing games. It had to go out. Although Ryan had never said anything before, she was too embarrassed to let him see how many packages of snacks she polished off.

She lifted the lid off the garbage can on the side of the house, and out of the corner of her eye she saw a man exiting his car in her driveway. Her movements slowed down to the point she had almost stopped moving. Quickly Jorie threw the bag in the huge plastic can, eyes still on the handsome stranger. As she walked over to him, she wiped her hands on her pants, wishing she had bothered to wear something decent that day.

"Hi," she said with a smile. "Can I help you?"

"Hey Bronx," came her husband's voice, seemingly out of nowhere. He had been working in the garage, and Jorie hadn't even realized he was there. He motioned at her. "This is my wife Jorie. Honey, this is Bronx. He's going to help me get that tree out of the yard before it falls on the cars."

Jorie's eyes met Bronx's, and though he smiled politely and nodded at her, she felt as though he could see into the very depths of her soul. Her face felt hot, and she thought every butterfly in the neighborhood had taken up residence in her stomach. She smiled back and mumbled "hi." Her head felt light, and it took her a minute to come back to the reality of the moment.

"It's right over here," said Ryan as he motioned towards the tree near their front window that had failed to produce any leaves that year. The two men walked toward it, and Jorie turned to go back into the house. It did not seem as though her husband noticed anything strange, but for Jorie it had been such a blood rush. She hadn't remembered feeling anything like that in years.

It took several minutes for Jorie to feel upright again. Just as she wandered towards the front window, ice cream bar in hand, Jack and Brennan tore though the room. Jack was pretending his arm was a laser gun and shooting his brother while running backwards. Jorie glanced out the large pane of glass at the muscular frame of the man who had just temporarily robbed her of her brain function. She was about to drift into a mental fantasy when the phone rang. Frustrated with the caller's rude interruption of her personal mental wandering, Jorie pulled herself away from the window and went to answer the phone.

* * * * *

Several weeks passed, and Jorie occasionally experienced a fleeting romantic thought here and there about Bronx. Even though she hadn't seen him since the first day they met in front of her garage, somehow she felt she would never forget the almost-icy blue of his eyes. She wasn't sure if it was real, or a feature she had concocted in her own mind, but she could have sworn he had a deep dimple in his left cheek.

Mostly though, she kept doing what she normally did. She took her kids to school, fed and played with them, took them to school functions, after-school programs, anything that would keep them busy.

Jorie truly loved her children, but at times she struggled with the demands of being a mom. Before she and Ryan were married, there seemed to be nothing more she wanted in the world than to have a child of her own. She had seen her friends get married, have kids, and essentially "grow up" while she was still trying to finish college and date men who were all wrong for her. When she met Ryan, it seemed exactly what she needed to get herself closer to that dream of having a family. Too many of her friends' marriages and relationships had ended because despite their initial excitement, most discovered that the men they thought were going to be great dads really just wanted to be young and party after all.

It wasn't like that for Jorie. Certainly she had met her share of deadbeats and party boys. She maybe would have even settled down with one of them had she been given the chance. She wasn't. Though she wouldn't fully admit it to herself, even now, they were mostly just interested in her for sex. Jorie appeared outwardly confident, but deep down she knew that most of her relations with males were less about any genuine interest in her and more about getting her into bed. At the time she told herself she was using them just as much, for companionship, for company, for a warm body to be next to. But the reality was a lot more about searching for that one person who was going to love her when they were both sober and had all their clothes on.

The latter was something that was a constant struggle for Jorie. She was never comfortable with her clothes off in any situation. Hell, she didn't even want to see herself in the mirror heading for the shower. How she was ever able to get naked with anyone around was amazing. More often than not, alcohol was involved. It was the coping method she had used around boys and men ever since high school. That was where she had discovered that her insecurities, about her weight, her skin, her hair, whatever other young adolescent girls can come up with to be critical of, would all just sort of disappear after a couple of beers. At 17 she had fallen in love for the first time. Jorie had never before felt so comfortable and nervous around somebody at the same time. He was a couple of years older, and though he still wasn't legal to drink either, they spent many nights drinking Dr. Pepper and Southern Comfort, warm from being kept in the glove box. Jorie didn't even care for it, but at least it took away the nervousness.

When she met Ryan at the restaurant where they both worked as servers, Jorie knew it was going to be different. He looked at her more like a buddy, like somebody he could have fun hanging out with. At first they were just friends, having drinks at the restaurant's bar when their shifts were over, or hanging out with other co-workers at the pool hall down the street from work. Ryan had left college and was living with a roommate who cooked at the restaurant as well. It seemed they were all together so often Jorie felt as though she had a new family, which was just what she needed at the time. Somehow it seemed natural that she and Ryan would end up as a couple. It was a position they slipped into without much fanfare or even discussion of what it meant. Jorie was glad to not have to "talk" about it much. She had spent her whole life with people asking her how she felt about things, wanting her to "talk" about everything. Her relationship with Ryan just went from friends to lovers in one breath, and it was the first time in a long time Jorie was able to have that sort of relationship with anyone sober.

Now they had just celebrated their 10th anniversary. Ryan had suggested a trip, maybe to Mexico or a cruise. Jorie thought of nothing she would have loved more, but refused. She just couldn't bear the thought of having to squeeze into an airline seat or buy new bathing clothes for the beach. Ha, the BEACH? Still with the same insecurities and about 80 pounds more weight, Jorie would have sooner had a stake driven through her foot than have to even seriously consider it. The truth was, Jorie adored the ocean. It was her body she had the issue with. She felt horrible that it was holding her husband back from having a great trip to celebrate all their years together. But as always, in his quiet way Ryan understood, and instead booked them a very nice suite at a beautiful hotel downtown. They spent one quiet, uninterrupted night there while some friends watched the kids. Much as the rest of their relationship, it was understated. No fireworks, just the same food, TV, and missionary position as at home, only for $200 a night.

Three

THESE THOUGHTS WERE CONSUMING HER one afternoon when she came across an ad in her email. It was from the hospital where her friend, Gina, was a nurse. Jorie had signed up for their email updates in order to read a story about Gina's fundraising work for children on the cancer floor.

There it was, in all capital letters next to the box she checked to delete it as junk mail. BARIATRIC PLAZA INFO MEETING TONIGHT. She had seen similar advertisements many times in her inbox, on TV, and in various other places on the net. For some reason, they had never seemed to catch her attention the way this one did. She felt compelled to open it.

Most of the email was just information; there was a meeting being held in the bariatric wing of the hospital, covering all aspects of the surgeries available and what each entailed. But near the bottom, in a small box on the left of the page was a video clip. Jorie clicked it.

"When I looked in the mirror I saw somebody I didn't recognize, and somebody I didn't want to be," said a woman, maybe in her early 40's looking healthy and fit. She talked for a couple of minutes about her life prior to her weight loss surgery, while pictures of her much heavier ran on the screen. Then they showed her much thinner, posing on a mountain-side on a hike, with a boy (probably her son) dressed for a formal dance, and in a swimsuit on a beach. Jorie just knew that it was in Mexico, even though she only saw it for a few seconds. This woman had been on Jorie's dream vacation.

The video ended with the woman describing how the changes she had gone through physically had completely changed the rest of her life. Jorie only half listened. She couldn't get the image of the woman she had first seen being so very much like herself, sitting on a beautiful, sun filled beach in an adorable pink swimsuit. It wasn't the woman, but the stunning background of the picture that had Jorie riveted.

After watching the video several more times, Jorie picked up the wall phone and called Gina.

"Hey, I saw an ad on your work website for a meeting tonight and wanted to see if you would go with me?" Of course Gina wanted more information, and when Jorie was done explaining, her friend agreed to come along for moral support.

Jorie then called Ryan to ask him to bring home dinner for the kids. She told him she was going with Gina to the hospital, but stopped short of telling him what the event was really about. He seemed confused about why she would go there, but he knew his wife didn't get out of the house much. If she had plans to spend time with her friends, he didn't want to question it.

Later, when Jorie entered the huge, spacious room where the information meeting was being held, she felt a sudden pang. She wasn't sure if it was guilt over not telling her husband what she was considering, fear over the prospect of having an elective surgery, or some other concern that she could not put her finger on. What could it be that made her so jumpy? This was only a place to get information, a place to ask questions and find out whether or not this might be for her. She hadn't committed to anything, and didn't have to. She could turn around and walk out at any time. She was about to suggest this very thing to Gina when a woman at the front of the room announced that they would be starting. It was time to sit down, and Jorie felt some of her anxiety subside.

She sat next to her friend, who was still dressed in her scrubs from work, listening to this woman describe the various types of weight-loss surgeries available. She talked about what they meant, which doctors performed them, and how the process worked to become eligible for the procedures themselves. Jorie was overwhelmed at first, a bit confused, and then downright sure this wasn't going to be the thing for her. What had she been thinking? An elective surgery that carried the same risks as many other surgeries people would normally avoid like the plague, with three little kids at home and a husband who depended on her for most almost everything? This just seemed too selfish to even consider as a possibility.

When the woman leading the meeting got to the end of her standard sales pitch, she told the 30 or so people in the room that they would be breaking into groups of about six. Jorie was about to turn to Gina for the second time that night and suggest they make a quiet exit when Jorie looked at the five people who were now standing at the front of the room. The woman on the end was the beach-goer she had spent the afternoon watching on the website video clip.

"Oh my God," she whispered to Gina. "I saw that woman on the hospital's website today. She looks amazing."

"Which one?" Gina asked.

"The one on the end in the blue jacket. She's lost, like, 200 pounds." Jorie could see the woman was standing at the front of the room, but all she could see behind her was the balmy beach and clear blue water.

The woman leading the meeting turned to the five people standing next to her. "These are some of our success stories from St. Keats' bariatric program, and they'll each be heading their own discussion group to give you a little more personalized view of what you can expect from this program. Please pick a group to start with, and we'll rotate about every ten minutes until you've all had a chance to meet with each of them. So let's each pick a place to start and get going."

Jorie was drawn to start with the video woman, but Gina steered her towards a tall man named Bill who was leading a group on the other side of the room. "Let's start with Bill's group. He works here at the hospital, and I know he's going to have some great information for you."

The women made their way to Bill's group and listened to him talk about the experience he had as a gastric-bypass patient. He had felt very isolated as a 400 pound man, but had lost half of his body weight, changed his career, and fallen in love with his current wife at a church event. His story was touching to Jorie, but not the "beach" story she longed to hear about from the woman across the room.

Finally about 40 minutes later Jorie and Gina were able to get to the group of people hanging on every word coming from the beach lady. Jorie soon learned her name was Laney, and that she had a procedure called a sleeve gastrectomy. Jorie heard a bit about what that was during the intro to the meeting, but hadn't yet decided on what kind of surgery she might want. Laney was in her late 40's, had grown up in a small town dealing with a weight problem since junior high school, and had been married three times. Jorie couldn't help but be drawn in by every word this woman said. She didn't even move on to the final group when their ten minutes were up.

During the last few minutes with each group there was time for questions, but everyone seemed to have at least two for Laney. One of the other potential patients asked Laney about how she came to represent the hospital in their TV ads and online. Jorie hadn't recognized her from television, probably because she had a tendency to fast forward through most commercials or ignore anything about weight loss products. Anything that highlighted people who lost a lot of weight made her depressed and drove her out to the kitchen to see what there was to eat.

Jorie hung back in the group, listening. She waited alone along one of the tall windows while Gina laughed and chatted with her co-worker who was leading one of the other groups. Most of the people had cleared out of the room when she found an opportunity to approach Laney alone.

"I'm sorry," she began, "I know we had an opportunity to ask you questions before." Jorie wasn't even really sure what it was she wanted to ask. There was a flood of questions she wanted to unleash, but she didn't know where to start. The beach picture flashed in her head, and that was all she could focus on. "Can you tell me where the picture was taken of you on the beach? The one that's on the hospital's website?"

Laney smiled at Jorie and continued to pack papers in her large purse. She tilted her head to the side. "It was in Cancun. My husband was going there for work, so we made it a little vacation. Have you been there?"

"No. I just..."

"You'd like to go there?" Laney interrupted.

"Well yes, I would." Jorie's thoughts were beginning to clear now, but Laney interrupted her again. She stopped what she was doing and turned in Jorie's direction.

"This idea of weight loss surgery is new to you, isn't it?" Jorie nodded. "I'm asking because people have a tendency to ask me a lot of unrelated questions rather than just asking what they want to know. What do you *really* want to know about the surgery?"

Jorie felt completely uncomfortable now, but this seemed to be the kind of now or never situation you found yourself in rarely, and regretted later when you let it get away. "I think I want this surgery, but I don't know. I don't know what my husband will think about it, I'm not sure it's safe. I have kids..."

Laney was shaking her head. At first Jorie thought she was going to chastise her, but then she realized Laney was still smiling. She relaxed.

"Those are all important things to think about. Nobody is going to know what the right decision is for you and your family. But I had to ask myself if it was worth going through my whole life in a body I hated, trying just one more diet, dealing with one more disappointment. It wasn't worth it to me, and I was lucky that my husband was very supportive. I was at the point where there were no more "diets" left in me. I had to do something to change everything about how I related to food and my very dietary habits, because just trying to eat healthy on my own or with some kind of program was not cutting it. If you feel like that, then I would give the surgery some serious consideration. If you feel like there is something else out there that can help you, then I would encourage you to keep looking for it. This whole process is worth every tough moment, but it's not the easy out everyone wants to label it as." Laney paused and smiled again. Jorie could see now why she was their spokesperson. "Does any of that cover what you were wondering?"

Jorie's eyes were huge, and she could only nod and try to swallow the lump in her throat. Everything she had been wondering about had cleared out of her head, and she felt like she had heard exactly what she had come for.

Laney went back to packing the things in her purse, picked it up and slung it over her shoulder. "I think you already know the answers you're looking for. Just keep asking yourself the questions and it will become clear. Call Dr. Cain's office. Her bariatric coordinator is incredible, but she can only give you facts. She can't give you the answers to the question of right or wrong. Start with the easy stuff. The rest will come to you when you know the basics."

In their entire marriage, Jorie had never lied to Ryan about anything she did; mostly because she rarely *did* anything. In her mind she had many unexpressed thoughts, feeling and desires. She figured this was normal. Who didn't have thoughts they never verbalized to their spouse? Her unexpected attraction to his friend

Bronx leaped to the forefront of her mind. She hadn't thought about him in months.

But this was different, Jorie told herself. This was something they'd obviously have to discuss, but she thought it better to wait until she could give him all the information she felt certain he would want to know.

A week later, Jorie had spent countless hours on the computer. She had researched every type of bariatric procedure there was, talked to numerous people online who had undergone the surgeries, and read up on every doctor in her area who performed them. She even called their insurance company to find out about their surgical coverage. She felt as prepared as she could to take the next step…talking it over with Ryan.

It was a Tuesday afternoon when the opportunity presented itself. Ryan was home early from work, Grace was napping, and the boys were playing in the neighbors' backyard. Jorie was nervous about bringing it up, but felt there never would be a "right" time.

She set the laptop on the kitchen table and said, "Honey, I have something I wanted to show you." She started with Laney's video. Ryan didn't seem nearly as impressed as she had been, but Jorie didn't let that deter her. She told him everything she had learned over the past few weeks; which surgery she wanted, how much it would cost, what the downtime would be, benefits and disadvantages of all of it. She wanted him to be on board, but she knew he would respond better if she was being completely honest. He was going to have doubts, but she was prepared to dispel any concerns he could bring up.

Jorie felt was rambling yet again, and decided to take a deep breath and see where they were. Ryan looked at her fairly seriously, a bit like she had just proposed having her body frozen so it could be thawed out far in the future. Oh, and she was doing it the following week, dead or not.

"So this surgery thing, you really want to do this? Don't you think it's kind of a dangerous risk to take, having an unnecessary surgery with three kids at home? Why do you want to take that chance, of something going wrong?" Ryan seemed to be taking her seriously, but he wasn't on board. She could tell from his voice.

"No, I thought the exact same thing. I know it seems a little crazy, but look at it statistically. It's a very safe procedure. I'm in more danger driving the kids to soccer, and you would never try to talk me out of that. It's just one overnight in the hospital and a week or so recovering at home." Jorie didn't want to sound like she was begging, but it was becoming clear that Ryan was going to need more convincing than she had estimated. Maybe she needed a new approach.

Jorie wanted Ryan to know how important this was without sounding desperate. She hadn't realized until just then how very much she wanted to have this done. "It's a lot to process. Do you want some time to think about it?"

Ryan kissed the top of her head, seemingly grateful to be let out of the conversation so easily. "I will think about it, but baby, I think you look just fine the way you are. Why fix something that ain't broke?" He headed upstairs to take a shower, leaving Jorie to ponder how her well-laid plans could have gone so completely in the wrong direction.

Four

TWO WEEKS LATER JORIE SAT in a large doctor's waiting room in a very large chair. All the chairs in the room were unusually big, and she let out an ironic little laugh under her breath. 'Nice, fat people chairs,' she thought to herself. So glad they thought of everything.

Jorie realized it was kind of nice to sit in something that didn't squeeze her thighs and pinch her as if it were trying to take her hostage. She glanced around at the other people waiting for their appointments. Most of them were in a similar boat. Only a couple of them looked like they could have fit comfortably in a conventional chair. She wondered if they were success stories of Dr. Cain's, or just there to support somebody considering bariatric surgery. Kind of like anti-obesity cheerleaders. The thought made her want to chuckle again, but was afraid of getting the same suspicious looks she had gotten the first time, as though she were a psych patient out on a day pass.

She herself did not have a cheerleader to be dwarfed by the exceptionally wide chairs and save her a spot while she met with the doctor. Ryan's promise to think over her surgical proposal seemed to have been dropped soon after his kiss on her forehead. That had been the end of it in his mind. She brought it up one time the previous week, but he mumbled that he couldn't hear her while he was working on the car. Jorie knew that was politely translated into, 'No honey, I didn't think about it and frankly don't want to discuss it right now, and I probably won't in the near future, and by the way could you please bring me a beer?'

But to Jorie, it was anything but a dead issue. She had made the doctor's appointment when she was sure she could convince her husband that this would be a great thing for not only her, but him, the kids, their relationship. When she discovered it would be a little harder to convince him than originally planned, she decided to go to the appointment anyway. Dr. Cain was a very well respected surgeon. It was only because of a cancelation, and her friend Laney pulling a few stings that she was even able to get in as quickly as she did. Jorie wasn't about to give it up just because her husband needed a bit more convincing.

"Jorie Asher?" came the nurse's voice from the open door leading to the back. Jorie was so lost in thought about how to get through to Ryan that she barely understood they were calling her until they said her name a second time. She gathered up her purse and coat and hurried to the nurse waiting patiently for her.

"Sorry, I wasn't paying attention," she said apologetically, head down as she followed the nurse.

The woman, a fit and young looking early 50, led her back to an exam room. "Oh, no problem. We have a lot of 'thinkers' out there. This is a pretty big decision." She seemed completely understanding, and put Jorie at ease right away.

The next three hours sped by as Jorie met with the bariatric coordinator, a nutritionist, social worker, nurses and the actual surgeon she hoped would agree to perform her procedure. It was mentally exhausting and physically depressing. She was shocked at every turn, having to face the reality of what she had done to her body over the years.

Her first stop was to get weight and height measurements. Though she was horrified about stepping on a scale in the privacy of her own bathroom, in this instance she tried to look on the bright side. Her insurance company would only pay a portion of the surgery if her body mass index was at a certain level. For the first time in her life, being "overweight enough" was going to pay off. She was inwardly disgusted with herself that her thinking had come to that point.

Jorie's next stop had her meeting with the center's social worker, though she didn't understand the necessity. The woman spoke with her for almost 45 minutes, asking her questions about her family, her husband, her history with food and what her plans were to deal with the aftermath of the surgical procedure.

"I'm not quite sure what you mean by that," Jorie said, confused.

The social worker, Janet, smiled knowingly. "Most people don't. We're finding that patients who don't have a good support system in place after they've returned home and have to learn how to deal with food differently often can experience other problems. Do you feel like you have a good support system?"

Jorie didn't realize they were going to require Ryan's support for her to go through with this. She wanted to answer honestly, without giving Janet a reason to not recommend her for surgery. "My husband is usually very supportive and helpful. I'm sure he'll do whatever he can to help with my food, and my recovery." She hoped she was telling the truth.

"How does he feel about you having this surgery?"

Jorie looked down at her hands, wringing them in her lap. This was the pointed question she didn't want to face. She didn't want to have to 'spin' this, but after all the work she had done she was paranoid that somewhere along this lengthy road there was going to be a hurdle she just couldn't get over.

"Well, we've talked about it. I think he has a few concerns about the recovery and stuff, so I thought it might be an easier decision for him once I had come to this appointment and had all the information."

Janet looked at Jorie with her head tilted slightly. "Why didn't he come with you?"

"He had to work," Jorie answered quickly. She was hoping this line of questioning was going to end soon. She started to feel like she was sitting in the principal's office, being questioned about vandalism in the locker rooms.

"Jorie, after you've had your surgery," Janet said, reaching into a card holder next to her computer, "you're going to need all the support you can get, not just from people in your family. Here is the information about our support group. It meets every other week. I've found that many of our patients never miss one if they can help it. It's an excellent way to meet with others who are going through many of the same things you will be experiencing, and learning ways to cope."

Jorie was confused again, and despite her desire to get out of this meeting as soon as possible, she felt she had to ask. "I'm sorry, you say cope like they've gone through a tragedy? I'd like to think I'm going to be pretty happy once this weight comes off."

"I think you will be too, but keep in mind that your life is going to change a lot after this surgery. You won't be able to relate to food in the same way, and we don't know how you're going to feel about that until the time comes." Janet crossed her arms on top of the desk and leaned closer to Jorie. "Trust me; the meetings will make it so much easier to learn what to do, and what not to.

This time she wasn't going to make this conversation last any longer than necessary. She didn't understand what Janet was talking about, relating to food and how to cope. Was she serious? Jorie just wanted to stop relating to food so damn often, and she felt like coping wasn't really going to be a problem.

Next she sat down with the nutritionist, who had told her to bring in a written record of all the food she had eaten over the past couple of weeks. Jorie was uncomfortable providing a stranger with the long list of meals, snacks and unhealthy things she had put in her mouth on a daily and sometimes hourly basis. It had been hard to keep track of, between the kids running off with her notebook and pen, and not wanting to face the reality of how many calories she was regularly consuming. She knew it was important though, and did manage to keep very good records to discuss at her appointment.

Finally was a meeting with Dr. Cain. She was not much older than Jorie, tall and slender with beautiful long brown hair. Jorie was taken aback at how attractive this woman was, and found it hard to imagine her with her hands inside of a body performing surgery. She was very welcoming with a warm smile as she walked into the room.

"Hi, Jorie," she said, checking the name in the file as she came in the room. "I'm Dr. Cain."

"I figured that, hi," Jorie smiled, holding out her hand to shake the doctor's.

They talked for several minutes about the meetings she had conducted with the other professionals in the clinic. Jorie was relieved to find that according to the nutritionist, social worker and nurse, she was qualified to be a surgical candidate. It hadn't occurred to Jorie until that moment that she was being interviewed. She had always thought of going to the doctor as looking to see what they could do to help you. In this case, it appeared to be more of *will* they help you. She was glad she hadn't known that in the beginning. It was entirely possible that she would have just stayed home. Interviews made her nervous.

"Jorie," Dr. Cain began, "it looks like this is something you've struggled with much of your life. Food, I mean. Is this correct?" She was reviewing the hand-written notes the social worker had stuck in the file.

Jorie nodded. "I do seem to have some problems with overeating." Who was she kidding? This was a bariatric doctor for crying out loud. It was probably the first person in her life with whom Jorie found comfort in discussing her 'food issues' (that's what her mother liked to call it). She had spent most of her adult years hiding the way she ate, the way she interacted with food from everyone she knew, even her husband. Here was the person she was counting on to help her towards the solution she had been chasing so long, and all she could say was that she might have a problem with overeating? Jorie almost chuckled at the irony of her own statement.

But what exactly could she say? Could she tell Dr. Cain about the stashes of candy she had around her house, mostly out of fear that her husband might find out how many chocolate bars she could actually eat or that her kids might find them and she might actually have to share them? Could she talk about how she would get up at night when everyone was asleep so she could polish off the leftovers from supper, or make herself a snack about the size of a regular meal during the hours she was supposed to be sleeping? How would the good doctor like to hear about Jorie's fast food binges while her daughter was asleep in the car and her boys were in school? Maybe she'd like to know that Jorie told her husband she was buying food for herself and the kids so he wouldn't know that she had actually spent all the money that showed up on the credit card statement on food just for her? Sure, Dr. Cain looked like she'd never had so much as a damn bite of anything with more than 90 calories in it, but Jorie was just certain that she'd love to hear all about her insane food habits. No, maybe her original statement about overeating problems was the way to go right now. She didn't think it was necessary to let the doctor in on all her dirty little secrets on their very first meeting. Not to mention, Jorie didn't feel she had the ability to say many of those things out loud anyway.

The doctor took off her fashionable glasses and looked directly at Jorie. "I have to tell you, this surgery is going to change the way you are able to eat. Your stomach is only going to be able to hold about two to three ounces of food in the beginning, and it's going to take some getting used to." As though she was reading Jorie's mind, the doctor added, "I know it sounds like I'm lecturing you. I am. This is not something you do as another "diet," Dr. Cain continued. "This *will* change many aspects of your life, and it's especially important that you do everything we lay out for you. That includes having a support system, preferably both at home and outside. Something like our hospital support group or whatever you think you're comfortable with. This is probably one of the few surgical procedures where the doctor doesn't necessarily try to encourage the patient to go forward with it. With necessary medical surgeries of course they're trying to save someone's life, and with a lot of plastics they'll promise they can make you look just like you want. But bariatric cases are different. That's why we make you jump through so many hoops." The doctor smiled at Jorie. "We need to make sure you know everything you need to be successful with this."

"I don't think I've researched anything so much since college," Jorie chuckled.

Dr. Cain nodded, still smiling. "That's good. It's good to be prepared, but remember not everything you need to know is going to be available online. Even if you have great support on there from other bariatric patients, please make sure you're working with your family, the hospital support group or me if you have any problems."

Jorie tried not to look too excited. "Does that mean you think I'll be able to have the surgery?"

Dr Cain nodded, flipping through Jorie's file. "Everything here looks good. You've met everyone you needed to and they all feel you'd be a fine candidate. So all that's left is having you set a date with Mara for the procedure itself."

The only thing that kept Jorie from jumping out of her seat and hugging the good doctor was the realization that she still had her husband to persuade. Despite the convincing performance she had put on for everyone in the surgeon's office, she knew the real battle was still waiting for her at home. This time she had no intention of letting Ryan off without giving her the answer she now felt she had to have.

* * * * *

And so it went, that after explaining the information she gathered from her appointment, Ryan was no longer able to blow off his normally agreeable wife with a simple "We'll see." She obviously meant business, and there was little that could be done to dissuade her. He knew she could be stubborn when she had her mind set on something, but Ryan hadn't seen her so adamant about anything since they were picking names for the kids. And even then, while he understood her desire to honor them through family names, it took some creative bargaining with Jorie in the hospital to keep his second son from being named Brenda.

An agonizingly slow month passed before Jorie lay in her pre-op bed, trying to look at anything in the room except her husband. He sat next to the bed, bouncing his leg up and down and rubbing his hands together, then stretching his arms over his head. His anxiety was making her crazy. She couldn't wait for the guy to get there with the gas and knock her out.

Nurses poked and prodded, interns checked her chart, and Dr. Cain stopped by to recap everything that was going to happen. When the surgeon left to go scrub up, it hit Jorie that she was almost there. As she watched the nurse preparing her for the operating room, tears ran silently down her cheeks.

The nurse noticed Jorie crying. "Are you alright sweetie? I know it can be overwhelming, but you have an incredible doctor."

Jorie wasn't worried about dying on the operating table. She didn't really know why she was crying. Maybe it was the seriousness of what she was about to do. Maybe it was the emotional exhaustion of all she had been going though crashing down on her. Maybe it was the relief of it finally happening. Probably all three. In any case, she wanted desperately to stop. The tears came faster as she worried they would think she was mentally unstable and cancel her surgery.

The nurse patted her arm just above the IV stuck in the back of her hand. "It's almost over, hon."

They wheeled Jorie's bed out of pre-op through the doors marked "Surgery". Ryan kissed her cheek right before she went in and told her he loved her. She knew he still wasn't alright with this, but it was out of his hands now. She smiled at him, hoping he knew how much she appreciated him. Several hospital staff lifted Jorie onto another bed, and she was pushed under a bright light. It was soon blocked by the kind face of a man in dark scrubs.

"Jorie, I'm Dr. Scott, the anesthesiologist." Hallelujah, the gas man was there!

Jorie woke up, groggy, with everything around her covered in white static. Her insides hurt like nothing she'd felt since childbirth. She asked the man sitting next to her bed, she assumed it was her nurse, for some medicine. He looked up at her briefly before he returned to his paperwork. Jorie thought she was asking, and then yelling for pain med. As quickly as she had awoke, she was back to sleep.

An hour later, Ryan's face appeared above her. "Hey honey, how are you doing?"

"Good," she croaked. Jorie actually had no idea if she was good. All she knew was the pain she'd woken up with before was gone.

The night went on with nurses and staff, coming and going. The next morning she was wheeled downstairs for a barium swallow test. Jorie almost threw up the foul-tasting liquid, and couldn't have been more grateful when it was over.

Dr. Cain came into her room later that afternoon. Everything had come back fine with her tests, and as long as she was walking fine on her own, Jorie could go home. She said she could probably run a marathon if it meant going home. She hated hospitals.

Ryan, who had gone home the night before to be with the kids, returned to pick her up. He carried down her bag and the flowers her best friend Gina brought by. They picked up her prescriptions for pain pills at the pharmacy and headed for the car.

"Wanna go to McDonalds?" Ryan joked.

"Very funny," she remarked, trying not to laugh at his dry wit for fear of busting open her new staples.

* * * * *

The first couple of weeks passed quickly for Jorie, who lay in bed most of the day, per her doctor's orders. She got up to walk every couple of hours, which had been recommended to avoid blood clots. Other than being tired, she felt pretty good most days. A couple of days after her surgery, she had a drain removed from her incision site. Three weeks out and she was being checked again at Dr. Cain's office.

"These look good," Dr. Cain remarked, checking the five small incision marks left by the procedure. "How have things been going at home? You're sticking to the food plan, and not lifting too much?"

Jorie had done everything by the book, though as she began to feel better she realized how different her life was in regards to food. Not wanting to be a disappointment to her surgeon, she nodded. "Everything is good. I'm eating mushy foods now, and haven't been lifting much. Gracie has been great about not making me carry her. I feel good."

"Have you been to any of the support group meetings?" the doctor asked.

"No, but hopefully I'll get to one this month. I haven't been doing much except getting better." This part was all true, though Jorie knew she probably wouldn't make it to a meeting. She didn't feel sitting around talking to a bunch of other people about her surgical experience was going to help her with her weight loss. For the time being, she just wanted to concentrate on recovering, in her own home and on her own terms.

Dr. Cain was writing in Jorie's chart. "Good, because it can be really valuable to your progress after surgery."

Jorie woke up each day excited to get on her scale. She knew the feeling from years of dieting. That "Monday morning weigh-in" feeling when you knew you'd stuck to your diet and had probably lost weight. Only this time every day she was finding herself down from a few ounces to several pounds. Though she was having a hard time seeing the physical changes, she could tell in the pictures Ryan took of her each week. The only thing she was as excited about as the scale was the pictures.

As the pounds came off and Jorie began to feel more like herself, she found the idea of old habits creeping back into her mind. Since the surgery left her with essentially a "new" stomach, she had to move from liquids to soft foods, and very slowly back to more solid things. Initially she had no desire to eat anything that wasn't part of the menu plan she and her dietitian had laid out. One afternoon, for no apparent reason she could figure, her thoughts wandered to a stash of candy bars she had hidden in the laundry room behind several boxes of light bulbs. Even though she knew she wasn't supposed to eat one, she found herself on a stool, moving aside the boxes and reaching inside the old shoe box for one of her favorite confections. The box was empty!

Jorie closed her eyes, knowing it was for the best but highly disappointed. She was far too embarrassed to ask Ryan about it when he got home. He had to have been the one who had cleared out all the candy, but Jorie couldn't bring herself to even admit it was there, let alone ask what he'd done with it. She knew she had no business considering anything with that much sugar. After all the convincing it had taken to get Ryan to consent to her surgery, there was no way she could admit to wanting a candy bar just weeks into her recovery.

Over the next few days Jorie discovered that all of her secret hiding places had been cleaned out. Ryan wasn't a big sweets eater, and she knew he would have never fed all that chocolate to the kids. No, he had most likely thrown it all in the trash. Jorie found this thought depressed the hell out of her. It was like having lost a good friend, and she mourned the loss of the food she had been so accustomed to keeping her "occupied" for most of her life.

One afternoon, Jorie was cleaning out the freezer when she came across a small pint of her favorite ice cream that even she had forgotten was there. Despite the fact that half of her frozen foods were melting on the counter, Jorie sat down at the table with a spoon and dug in. She didn't make it half way through the remaining ice cream when it all came back up on her. Jorie knew this was a very real possibility when she started, but just couldn't stop herself. Her eyes watered as she threw up, and she knew that her days of eating like she had previous to her surgery were over. Again, it was like hearing of the death of a loved one, and Jorie sat on her bathroom floor and sobbed.

After three more episodes of overeating, Jorie considered the possibility that she might need some help. Though she was hesitant, she made plans to attend the hospital's support group meeting the last Thursday of the month. It was similar to the information meeting she had first gone to when preparing for her surgery, but with mostly post-op bariatric patients. Jorie was nervous, but relaxed when she saw Laney was there. Laney smiled at her, and nodded in recognition. This put her a little at ease, though she still felt an overwhelming desire to run from the room once the meeting started.

People went around and introduced themselves, talking about the surgery they had undergone and how long it had been. They discussed how they were doing, but Jorie kept her intro brief. She was terrified to admit her recent slip-ups in front of all these strangers. They all seemed to be doing so great after their surgeries, and Jorie was sure they would think she was a miserable screw up. After years of trying to blend, of going mostly unnoticed, she found she preferred herself this way.

Half way through the meeting, after hearing about so many success stories and seeing the positive results her fellow patients were experiencing, Jorie felt her face get hot and her breathing speed up. She needed to get out of the room. The walls seemed to be closing in on her, and the ceiling actually looks like it was lower than when she entered the room. She felt dizzy as she quickly made her way to the exit. Once in the hallway, Jorie sank into a chair and put her head down on her knees.

"Little panic attack maybe?" asked Laney as she came out of the meeting room. Jorie looked up at her, embarrassed that the woman who had so inspired her to go forward with her surgery was now seeing her in this state. "Don't worry, it will pass. Always does." Laney sat down in the chair next to Jorie. "I've been around here quite a few years, and one thing you can always count on is that people will react in all sorts of different ways after their surgery."

Jorie wasn't sure what to say. Part of her believed Laney was the person who might best understand what was going on with her. Another part of her was certain Laney would be mortified at Jorie's inability to stick to her post-op plan or make a real commitment to losing the weight. She figured it was better to just keep it to herself for the time being.

Laney wasn't waiting for Jorie to make any startling confessions. "Come back in whenever you're feeling up to it." With that, Laney patted Jorie on the shoulder and went back to the meeting. As Jorie watched her go, she didn't know if she would ever feel 'up to it.' She finally rose from the chair, looked at the meeting room door and walked directly to the elevator that went down to the parking garage. She leaned against the inside of the elevator, determined that she would do this on her own.

Five

THERE WAS A BUZZ IN the house as Jorie and Ryan got things together for their barbeque. Jorie was especially nervous. She had been having a tough time dealing with the aftermath of her surgery, but found that her spirits were lifted being surrounded by people, especially people who hadn't seen her new form. She couldn't believe how different she felt just eight months out. Of course she figured being down 100 pounds didn't hurt.

Jack and Brennan came tearing through the kitchen, and Jorie was able to raise her arms just quick enough to avoid them taking out the entire tossed salad she held in her hands. "Slow down," she yelled after them, but they were off through the patio door. Jack yelled an off-handed "Sorry, mom" back at her, only to be echoed by his younger brother. Jorie could hear Jack tell Brennan not to copy him, and smiled as she heard the insanity ensue from there. She remembered playing the 'don't copy me' game with her sister when they were young, and it made her grateful that her kids had each other.

Ryan walked into the kitchen with a plate of uncooked hot dogs prepared for the grill. He kissed her on the cheek as she chopped the veggies for the burgers. "Gracie sleeping?" he inquired. She nodded. "I think everything is pretty much ready. Oh! I forgot to get the big table out of the garage." He headed through the doorway again just as the doorbell rang.

People poured in over the next 20 minutes, many of whom Jorie had seen as recently as that week but still marveled at her amazing transformation. She blushed, smiled, and shook her head when they said she was getting too thin. She still had 50 pounds to lose, so she knew they were either being polite, or just weren't used to seeing her at this weight.

Ryan was busy working the grill, and most people were in the backyard either watching the kids play in the above-ground pool or on the swing set when the doorbell rang a final time that day. Jorie wiped her hands on a dish towel as she made her way to the door, dodging Jack and his friend Alex who were headed back out to the pool. She was looking back at them as she opened the door to let in their next guest.

When she looked up, Jorie's face got instantly hot and her stomach dropped into the bottoms of her feet. She had no time to even wonder why this kept happening to her with this man, as Bronx's large white smile made every thought fly from her mind like doves being released from a cage.

"Hey," he said brightly, holding up a wine bottle, "I have no idea if you guys drink this stuff, but it seemed like an appropriate gift for the hostess." He dropped his arm back to his side, and held up a 12 pack of beer with the other. "In case the wine didn't go over." His blazon smile made Jorie blink her eyes.

She gestured at his hands. "Both look great. Come on in." She backed away sideways to let him in through the doorway. Bronx stepped in on the Venetian tile and handed the bottle to Jorie.

"Wow, you look great, very different." As soon as the words were out of his mouth, he looked as though he wished he could take them back. "I'm sorry, that sounded awful. I didn't mean it that way." His handsome face turned a bit red, leading Jorie to believe that even if he didn't mean it that way, it probably was really how he felt.

She smiled at him. "It's alright, and thank you." She went to close the door as he took off his leather jacket. She thought it was a bit warm for that heavy of a coat, when she noticed the Harley Davidson at the end of the driveway. "Is that your bike?"

Bronx glanced out the crack of the door she was peeking through. "Yeah, that's mine. Do you ride?" The question made Jorie let out a laugh that she thought was dangerously close to a snort.

"God no, but I love bikes. Maybe someday…" she trailed off.

"I'm happy to take you for a ride some time if you'd like." Again, his face turned crimson and they both laughed. "OK, I think I'm just going to stop talking for today. I meant…"

But Jorie didn't let him finish. "I got it, I got it," she giggled. She put her hand on his upper arm to direct him into the kitchen. Touching him in this way made the butterflies start back up in her stomach as she felt the muscles through his thin motorcycle t-shirt.

Ryan was thrilled to see Bronx walk into the backyard where he was flipping barbecued chicken. Jorie found her husband's friendship with this man a bit odd. She didn't know why. Maybe it was because she had never known Ryan to have a friend who'd ever even ridden on a motorcycle, let alone owned one. They seemed somehow mismatched. Jorie momentarily considered that these differences may have been the basis for her affinity for this man. She couldn't grasp why, but this thought disturbed her.

As the afternoon went on, Jorie had a harder and harder time concentrating on what her guests at the barbeque were talking about. She found her gaze drifting around the yard, searching Bronx out. After the third time he caught her looking at him, she realized she had better at least look like she had something better to do with her time. He was going to think she was coming on to him!

"Do you want a glass of wine?" Jorie asked Gina as she pushed herself out of her favorite lawn chair.

"Yeah, are you having some? I thought you weren't supposed to drink for a few more months?" Gina was asking, but with a hint of warning in her tone.

Jorie shook her head up and down. "I know, I know, but I don't think a little glass of wine is going to be a big deal." The truth was she had spent the whole afternoon wishing she could have a drink. She had never thought of herself as possessed, but she thought the alcohol might stop the voices screaming in her head that HE was here, actually here in her own backyard. The conflicting feelings were really killing her good time.

Two glasses of wine later, Jorie felt a bit dizzy. Even though she still wasn't able to take in the female conversations taking place around her, at least she wasn't staring at Bronx the whole time. She forced herself to focus on the rim of her wine glass, listening to Gina go on about the drama occurring at the hospital surrounding some new interns.

"Jorie!" The sound of her husband's voice hollering across the yard snapped her to attention. She looked over to the crowd of men near the grill, and bolted across the green grass. When she reached the group, she realized what was going on.

"Do we have the first aid kit?" Ryan asked, holding her good dish towel around Bronx's hand.

"Geez Ryan, what did you do to him?" she asked, seeing the blood seeping through the towel.

Ryan looked paler than Bronx, who had suffered the actual injury. "I didn't mean to. The knife just slipped when I was slicing the steaks…" His voice wavered, and he looked as though he might actually pass out.

Gina came up behind Jorie to see about the commotion. She unwrapped the towel and looked at the cut on Bronx's hand. "You might need some stitches in that. You really should have it looked at. Jor, don't you have a walk-in clinic near here?"

Bronx shook his head and re-wrapped his injured hand. "No really, it's not a big deal. I just need a good band-aid or some gauze. Just point me to that first aid kit."

Jorie laughed at the idea of him trying to bandage his right hand by himself. "I don't think so. Come with me, I'll get you something for it." She led him into the house, stopping to look in the powder room medicine cabinet for the first aid kit they kept there. It was gone, of course. Ever since Jack had learned to move a stool in front of any cabinet that might hold treasures for him, nothing in their house was safe from his grasp. "Come upstairs," she instructed, "I have some tape and gauze my kids haven't used to triage their GI Joes yet."

In her master bathroom, standing so close to Bronx made Jorie's heart beat faster again. The seriousness of the situation had done little to detract from her overwhelming attraction to him. A year had passed since the first time they actually met in her driveway, and she felt as though not a day had gone by. It was as though they had been madly, passionately in love in some previous life, brought back together in some cruel twist where she was married to another man.

Jorie leaned her hip on the counter, opening a large gauze piece from the paper while Bronx held his cut hand under the running faucet. "I don't know why I'm surprised, I'm sort of accident prone. This sort of thing seems to happen to me a lot. Even when I'm just sitting there, injuries just seem to find me." He was talking a bit fast, as though he was nervous himself. Jorie figured it was the scare of almost having her husband slice his hand off in their backyard.

"Seems like an odd thing for a biker," she said, smiling at him.

Bronx let out a laugh, acknowledging the irony. "I know, huh?" He took his hand out from under the water to examine it, and immediately it began to bleed again. Jorie quickly put a clean towel over it, holding it tightly.

"You should keep pressure on it, to stop the bleeding." She looked into his crystal blue eyes, just inches from her face. They seemed portals to a dimension she wanted desperately to visit, soon and often.

He was looking at her as well, and took a step backwards. "Thanks," he mumbled as he took over the pressure on his injury. "Maybe we should wrap it before I wreck all the towels in your house."

Jorie shook her head. "No worries, we have an endless supply. I can tell you on laundry day it's like we have two towels for everyone in town that need to be washed. I think they're multiplying in my dryer, maybe they're being made out of all the missing socks while they're tumbling in there, I don't know." Jorie was rambling like an idiot. What the hell was she even saying? There was no keeping her thoughts in order with him in the room.

Bronx laughed out loud at her analogy, and it made Jorie relax. She didn't want to make him uncomfortable, but she felt as though being close to him was the place she was meant to spend her life. It was a frightening thought. She loved her husband, had children with him, and had made a commitment to spend her life with *him*. It was maddening to have these feelings for someone else, Ryan's friend, and for no real reason she could make out.

"OK, let's see how it looks," Jorie said, reaching for his hand. She had the tape and other supplies ready to bandage him up, but looked at the deep gash, still bleeding. "Maybe Gina was right. You might need stitches in that. Are you sure you don't want Ryan to drive you over to the walk-in clinic? It's right around the corner?" Jorie didn't want to see a single scar on that perfect body.

"No really," he assured her. "I've been through much worse, it will be alright. If this doesn't help," he gestured toward the various medical supplies she had lined up on the counter, "I'll go in to my regular doctor tomorrow."

Jorie wasn't convinced, but tilted her head sideways and began bandaging the wound. "OK, your call." As she placed the last piece of tape, she chuckled softly. "I don't remember the last time I did this without having to kiss the boo-boo." She was mostly thinking out loud, but Bronx was amused as well.

"Go for it, couldn't hurt," he said, half joking. But when Jorie looked up from her medical patch job, she saw he had an intent look on his face that was completely serious.

Jorie raised his injured hand to her lips, eyes shut, and ever-so gently kissed the skin next to where she had just bandaged. He turned his hand slightly, stroking her cheek. When she finally had the courage to open her eyes and meet his brilliant blue gaze, he moved his hand behind her neck as if to pull her closer to him.

Ryan's voice came from the hallway, shattering the tempestuous moment like thin glass on concrete. Bronx immediately dropped his hand, and Jorie turned away from him, collecting items to be thrown away off the counter.

"Hey, there you guys are. I was worrying you were on the phone with your attorney plotting your upcoming lawsuit." Ryan laughed as he said it, and Bronx forced a smile of reassurance at his friend.

"Never happen, man. You know I wouldn't take anything of yours." Bronx looked pointedly at Jorie, but she couldn't bear to glance at him for more than a second. Her pulse was racing, and she felt as though she had almost made the biggest mistake of her life. She also felt immensely disappointed that it hadn't happened.

"Alright then, all patched up?" Ryan asked. Bronx held up his hand to show what Jorie had done, and Ryan nodded approvingly. "Great, let's have a beer. You probably lost a lot of fluids there. We should replenish." The two men left the bathroom together, Bronx behind Ryan. He looked back over his shoulder at Jorie.

She didn't dare look up. She didn't know if it was out of fear that he wouldn't look at her, or that he would. Either way, she felt this was as close to cheating during her marriage as she ever wanted to get again. The guilt was too much, as was Bronx's mental power over her. She vowed right then she would make every effort to stay as far away from him as she possibly could.

Just then Gina came into the bathroom carrying both of their glasses of wine. "Are you coming back down or what?" she asked, handing her friend's wine to her.

Jorie collected herself as she took the drink. Holding it up to Gina she said "You know it. Let's party."

Six

THE FOLLOWING WEEK WHEN RYAN returned to work, Jorie was so sick to her stomach she nearly threw up twice the first day he was gone. Bronx often did electrical work in the shop with Ryan, but she didn't know if he was there every day. The best she could tell he was an independent contractor, and only worked there when they needed something specific done. She didn't know which days that week, if any, he would be working with her husband, and she was completely terrified that he would tell Ryan what happened the night of their barbeque.

When Ryan returned from work the first day, he was in his usual mood. He walked in the house, gave Jorie her usual cheek peck, and proceeded to the couch where he played video games with Jack. Jorie listened intently to his tone when he spoke, trying to determine how much he knew. He had never been good at keeping things inside. If he had any idea what happened between Bronx and his wife, she would surely hear some sense of it in his voice.

Each day that went by Jorie felt more confident that not only did Ryan not suspect anything, but that Bronx was never going to say anything to him. He'd been to work at the shop on several occasions, but each day Ryan returned from work with the same benign reaction. Though it was tough not to ask too many questions about this man who so consumed her thoughts on a daily basis, she was too worried that her husband would catch on to the why. She had dodged a bullet the night of their barbeque, and didn't want to make things worse by calling Ryan's attention to her feelings for Bronx. There seemed no point.

Regardless, thoughts of Bronx bounced around in her head for weeks. Disappointment mixed with relief at how the situation ended, but neither lasted long. She was cooking marinated chicken breast and asparagus for dinner when Ryan came in from work. He screwed up his face at the menu.

"What? It's going to be good," she assured him. It had been an ongoing dispute between them ever since her surgery. Even though it hadn't quite been a year, Jorie was almost down to her goal weight. She intended to continue her healthier lifestyle permanently, or until her family threw her out of the house.

"If you say so," Ryan countered, obviously unconvinced.

Jorie shook her head, but didn't say anything. She wondered how long it was going to take for Ryan to accept the way things had changed in their house. Even though he had reluctantly agreed to the surgery, he seemed completely put off by many of the changes that resulted from it.

"How was work?" she asked, hoping a change of subject would lighten the mood. She was also hoping to hear some mention of Bronx, though she would never admit so, even to herself.

"It was alright. I think I got you a job." Jorie barely looked up from the salad she was tossing as Ryan continued on. "You remember Bronx? He was in all day fixing our shop wiring. Anyway, he's got a place downtown that could use some work."

Jorie's pulse sped up. She stopped what she was doing, looked out the window and blushed as she recalled the night in her bathroom months before. Although she'd been doing jobs here and there for her old decorating firm, it had never occurred to her this might lead to an encounter with Bronx. She was disturbed that her mind went immediately to that ideation.

"You told him I would do it?" She feared if she looked at her husband, her face would give away the secret she'd been carrying around, cherished and terrifying at the same time.

"Yeah sure, well you're really good at what you do. And you said the firm wasn't giving you very much work right now. The money would be helpful and I'm guessing he would feel better about having somebody he knows helping him. He's not really a "decorating" kind of guy. I think he just wants something to make the place homier." Ryan went about putting away his things from work, not noticing that his wife had not only frozen like a statue, but really wasn't listening to him.

Jorie started moving again slowly, like a cold motor. "I don't know."

"Come on Jor, it took me all day to convince him. Don't make me look like an ass."

Jorie looked at Ryan for the first time. "What do you mean it took you all day?"

Ryan chuckled. "I don't know, I think he was embarrassed about the whole idea of having a decorator at all. He turned about three shades of red when I mentioned it. But he's good with it now, so I think you should do it. Why not, right?"

The 'why nots' were so abundant Jorie couldn't even begin to count.

"Alright, well have him call the office and set up a time with Shirley." Jorie was already mentally preparing for how she was going to pass this off on one of the other decorators who did contract work through her firm. She knew Brittan did great work with downtown décor, but she was pretty attractive. Maybe George...

Ryan grabbed the remote and headed to the family room connected to the kitchen. "Actually, I thought you could go by after supper tonight."

"What? Seriously, tonight? Why?" Jorie heard her voice go up five octaves.

"I thought it would be good. He's not always sure what his schedule's going to be like, so you'll probably have to go in the evening anyway. I'm here with the kids. And why share the commission with your firm? You can do outside work on your own, right?" Ryan asked.

"Yeah I guess, but…"

He didn't let her finish. "Good, because I think it would be good for both of you." Ryan turned his attention to the TV, their discussion of her helping Bronx decided. Jorie was excited, but at the same time afraid it might not be good for any of them.

Three hours later she pulled up to the address Ryan had given her at home. Jorie figured she had set a record preparing dinner, feeding three kids and a husband, showering, doing her hair and makeup. She was grateful to have found some cute new business work outfits the week before. Ryan chuckled when he saw her getting ready in the bathroom.

"Professional is nice, but I don't think Bronx really cares how you look. He's not really a client, he's a friend."

Jorie ignored him, grateful that he interpreted her primping as an attempt at looking business-like rather than sexy.

As she rode up the elevator to Bronx's apartment on the top floor, Jorie was impressed at the details of the old building. This was not exactly where she expected him to live. She tried concentrating on the intricate carvings in the wood to keep her mind off her nervousness.

Jorie's hand shook as she reached for the buzzer outside Bronx's door. When he opened it a few seconds later, her whole body began to shake as well.

"Hi."

"Hey." When he smiled at her, the light from the hallway bounced off his white teeth.

Jorie was surprised to see he was even better looking than she had remembered. He was clean shaven, dressed like he was going out and smelled incredible. His whole home smelled like cologne and man. The aroma made the hairs on the back of her neck stand up. It wafted out into the hall as soon as he opened the door. Jorie's feet were welded to the floor where she stood, but the amazing smell and sight of this man who had consumed her thoughts for so long drew her forward into the apartment.

She stuttered as she walked past him. "I uh, Ryan said I was supposed to, you needed..." Jorie couldn't collect her thoughts enough to get the sentence out, but Bronx knew what she meant.

"Yeah, yeah, he thought you might be able to help me get this place fixed up." When Bronx closed his front door, Jorie finally looked up and began to take in the atmosphere. Her eyes widened as she saw the entire open loft with vaulted ceilings, flowing spaces and hardwood floors.

"Wow, this place is beautiful. How long have you lived here?" she asked as she moved slowly into the living space. There was no separation between it and the kitchen, and a large staircase lined the side wall.

Bronx walked with her, rubbing the back of his neck. "Um, about a year. My dad passed away and left it to me. He never did much with the place either. I think he just liked the view," he said as he walked to the wall of windows opposite the doorway.

Jorie set her portfolio on the simple coffee table and walked to the windows as well. Speechless, she shook her head at the beauty of the city lights twinkling in every direction. She finally dared glance at Bronx, who was gazing out the window, apparently lost in thought. "I can see why," she said softly. As his blue eyes met hers, she felt compelled to break the spell he had over her sooner rather than later. She turned and picked up the portfolio folder she had set down and carried it to the kitchen table.

"I brought with some pictures of some places I've done recently, so I want to see what you think you might want to do in here with..."

When Bronx's hand slid across her waist and onto her stomach, every nerve in Jorie's body fired. He kissed her neck, causing her to tilt her head and close her eyes. A shiver went down her back, spiking at the bottoms of her feet. His hot breath moved up her neck to her ear, which he pulled on gently with his teeth.

"Just tell me to stop," he whispered.

Was this a dare? If he had been counting on her good judgment to stop this before it went too far, he was going to be disappointed. There was so little brain function going on inside her at that moment, she couldn't have fought her way out of a paper bag if her life depended on it.

Jorie reached her hand up and laced her fingers through his dark brown hair. Even though she loved the feeling on her neck, she had dreamt about Bronx's lips for months. She turned, looking him dead in his glassy blue eyes. She wanted him to know how much she wanted him, and that she had no intention of telling him to stop.

His lips met hers, and they melted together like they had been cut out of a matching mold. Jorie hadn't kissed another man since before she met Ryan, and for a split second worried that she might not remember how to do it. Bronx quickly reassured her this would not be a problem, with a deep wet kiss that was so overpowering her jaw almost locked up. No, she hadn't forgotten how to kiss. She'd only forgotten what it was to be so overcome with passion that all reason flew out the window.

Without taking his lips off hers, Bronx bent down and picked Jorie up behind her knees. Even after having lost so much weight, Jorie would have normally felt uncomfortable being held by anyone. But somehow in his arms, she felt as light as air. He carried her into his dim bedroom as though she was a feather pillow.

Bronx laid her on the bed, gently lying on top of her, still kissing, moving his hands from her side to her hips to her thigh. With one quick motion he unbuttoned the short dress jacket she had on, exposing the thin white silk of the cami she wore underneath. He ran his fingers from her throat, down over her breast bone and gently underneath her shirt. Jorie froze, pushing his hand away without realizing she was doing it so forcefully.

Bronx snapped back to reality. "I'm sorry. What is it?"

Jorie looked to the wall, afraid if she looked at him the tears she could feel welling behind her eyes would come bursting out. "I, I'm sorry. I don't want you to stop." Jorie knew she had to look at him. "It's…my body." She didn't know how to say what she had to say. She sighed. "It's not exactly swimsuit issue material, if you know what I mean. My skin, after my surgery…" Jorie felt terrible to be wrecking this moment, but she had never realized just how uncomfortable it would make her having another man see the excess skin and stretch marks she had become so accustomed to.

Bronx smiled at her, brushing a lock of hair off her cheek. Shaking his head he said, "I don't care about that. I just want you," he almost whispered, placing a tender kiss on her lips.

The words sounded to Jorie like a line she would have heard from some frat boy in college. However, the sentiment behind it was so genuine, it relaxed her a bit. He was looking at her with every ounce of desire she had ever seen, and knew this had already gone to a point she couldn't and didn't want to stop. As he began to assure her they could stop, that he didn't want to do anything she was uncomfortable with, Jorie put a finger to his smooth red lips. Without a word, she moved his hand to her inner thigh and pulled his face towards her.

Slowly and carefully, Bronx began taking off Jorie's clothes as though she were made of glass. She didn't know if he was always this gentle, or if she'd scared him with her previous concern. Either way, it didn't matter. She couldn't think of anything other than the stretched muscles of his back she could see as he kissed her neck, breasts, stomach. He touched every inch of her body, and didn't seem deterred by any of it. When he entered her, she raised her hips to meet his and they moved together as they had choreographed and practiced this for years. Jorie's back arched, encapsulated by the first orgasm she'd had during actual sex in years.

When they collapsed in a sweaty heap on the pillows, both were breathing so heavy neither could speak. After several minutes Bronx recovered, taking her hand as he turned his head to look at her.

"Are you hungry?"

Jorie laughed out loud and narrowed her eyes. "What?"

"I think I've got something," Bronx said, jumping out of bed and putting on a pair of black boxers before quickly exiting the room. Jorie couldn't get the smile off her face as she lay in his bed, staring at the ceiling high above her head. She turned over on to her stomach, and realized there was another bank of floor-to-ceiling windows across from the bed. Even though they were uncovered, she felt it was unlikely anyone could see in them from this high up. She put her chin on her hand and looked out at the same beautiful view of lights she had seen in the living room.

Bronx came back in the room with a bottle of wine, two glasses and a small plate of cheese and grapes. Jorie had to laugh again. "What, do you watch soap operas or something?"

Bronx looked down at the fare in his hands. "Actually, the grapes and cheese are two of about six things I have in my fridge, but the wine I did pick up on the way home from work today. I think it's the same kind you were drinking at your house when I was there," he said looking at the bottle. He set the plate on the bed where Jorie was still laying on her stomach and had pulled the sheet over the middle of her body. Bronx poured her a glass of wine, handed it to her and put the bottle on the nightstand.

"Aren't you going to have some?"

He lay down on the bed, kissing her shoulder as he moved the plate out of his way. "Nope, I don't drink wine. Gives me a headache."

"Then why two glasses?" she wondered aloud.

He looked at the extra glass he'd set down with the wine and shook his head. "I really don't know, guess I wasn't thinking straight."

Jorie held her arm off the end of the bed, swirling her wine around in the glass. Her mind was settled for the first time since she could remember, but she knew it was the proverbial calm before the storm. She decided to soak it up as long as possible.

Bronx laid next to her on the low platform bed, popping grapes in his mouth and staring at the ceiling. Their feet touched, as though they couldn't stand being so close together without being physically connected somehow.

"I like brown," he said matter-of-factly.

Jorie looked over at him with her eyebrows furrowed. "What?"

"Brown. You know, the color?" Bronx popped another grape in his mouth. "And blue or black. And I don't like a lot of stuff all over. No knick knacks or a bunch of furniture nobody's allowed to sit on."

"Oh, you're talking about decorating," Jorie laughed. "You mean you really didn't just invite me over for this?" gesturing at her form silhouetted beneath the sheet.

Bronx rolled on his side and kissed her shoulder once again. "As I recall, I didn't really invite you at all. Ryan hounded me about it all day after I mentioned doing something with this place. I didn't know you were a decorator. To tell you the truth, I was kind of trying to avoid you."

Jorie didn't like where this was going. "Why?"

"Because I knew if I was alone with you I would probably do something I would regret."

"Do you regret it?" Jorie almost whispered, concentrating on the wine glass so she wouldn't have to look at him.

He contemplated it for a minute, not as though he wanted to say what she wanted to hear It was more like he wanted to give her a completely honest answer. "No, I don't. I'm not real proud of myself. Ryan is my friend. But I don't know what it is about you." He stopped short. Either he didn't know what else to say, or was afraid of saying too much.

When Jorie heard her husband's name, a shot of electricity went through her brain. It was like remembering something so awful from your past that your mind could only handle it for a split second. She knew it was the beginning of immense guilt for what she'd just done. She'd changed her marriage, her relationship with Ryan forever. Jorie pushed it out of her mind for the time being, enjoying the brief reprieve from the impending pain she knew was coming.

An hour later she had showered, enjoyed one last long stomach-churning kiss, and headed home. She quietly slid into bed next to her husband who was sound asleep. He barely moved, and she sighed, relieved to not be dealing with reality for a few hours. She felt like someone who'd been run down by a bus. Right now the adrenaline was keeping her from feeling it, but she knew it was going to hurt like hell in the morning.

Pouring cereal for the boys the next day at breakfast, Jorie didn't even hear the phone ring. She was yelling at Brennan for spilling yogurt on his school shirt, and the sound of Gracie crying was about to make her snap. When Ryan kissed her cheek as she was making coffee, she practically jumped out of her skin. Every unbearable emotion she was feeling over her indiscretion from the night before was being taken out on her family. Just great.

"Jorie, it's Bronx!" Ryan said, irritated. She was terrified that he knew what had happened, but quickly realized he was just frustrated that she hadn't heard him calling her name.

"Hello?" Jorie's voice was barely above a whisper.

"Hey," came his deep voice. "I swear I'm not a stalker. I just wanted to let you know you left your briefcase thing here." He was upbeat, and despite feeling she was the worst person to ever walk the earth, the sound of Bronx's voice lifted her spirits a tiny bit.

"Oh shit!" Her portfolio. She could see it sitting open on his kitchen table, where she'd left it right before they...

"Mom, don't say that word!" Jack commanded.

"Sorry buddy," she said, covering the mouthpiece with one hand. "OK, alright, I'll have to come get it." Jorie had an appointment at her firm that afternoon. Despite how unsure she was about being alone with Bronx again, she needed that portfolio.

Two hours later she'd dropped her kids off at school and daycare, and headed back downtown. To the 'scene of the crime,' as she now referred to it. All the guilt she felt earlier in the day seemed to wane as she got closer to his place. The fact that any of it was fading so soon after making love to another man actually scared her. What kind of person was she anyway? Didn't she care about her husband, her family, their life together?

For the second time in less than 24 hours she was riding the elevator to Bronx's loft, her hands shaking and her breath shallow. She should have asked him to meet her down at her car. Then she could have just taken the portfolio and left. Going up was a bad idea, but she didn't know how to stop herself.

Jorie had barely rung the bell when the door opened. Though she had told herself she was going to smile, be cordial and make this quick, she now found it impossible to even look up at Bronx. She managed a weak "Hey," eyeing her portfolio on the table near the kitchen.

"Hey, come on it," he said cheerfully. She could feel him smiling at her, even without looking. She didn't dare even steal a glance at his gleaming blue eyes. Jorie walked immediately to the table and reached for the handles on her case. Though she had every intention of going right back out the door, she froze. He was right behind her.

"Jorie?" he said softly. The sound of her name on his voice caused goose bumps on her entire body. She turned to go, hoping he wouldn't try to stop her, praying at the same time that he would.

"I have a meeting with a client, so…" she stammered, her eyes still averted.

"OK," Bronx said calmly. When she didn't move, he ducked a bit, trying to catch her gaze. As he put a hand on her arm, he began saying, "I was just wondering if you were alrig…"

Jorie shook off his hand and finally looked him square in the eye. "I can't leave my family!" she blurted, cutting him off. Her heart almost pounded right out of her chest, and though she meant every word she said, she almost wished she could take it back.

Bronx was taken aback. "I would never ask you to. Is that what this is about?"

She laughed sarcastically. "Yeah, that's what this is about," she said, nodding. "That's exactly what this is about. I'm married, I have children. My husband is your friend." Jorie was worried she was bordering on hysteria, but she couldn't seem to filter what was coming out of her mouth. "*I* am a horrible person! What I did was unforgivable and I can't take it back, but I don't have to make it worse. I have to think about my kids. I can't leave my family, so yeah, that is what this is about."

Bronx narrowed his eyes, pain crossing his face. He finally nodded. "I understand. I really wasn't trying to cause you problems, though obviously I did. I'm sorry," he said sincerely.

Jorie couldn't have asked for a worse response. She was hoping he would be an ass, call her a name, tell her it was her own damn fault for screwing up her marriage in the first place. Any of the things she had been telling herself that morning would have been acceptable. But this she didn't expect. This made her feel horrible, and worse, it made her want him even more.

Her voice softened. "No, I'm sorry. I didn't mean to freak out. Damn it!" she said, walking around him and grabbing her hair in her hands. She turned back towards him, shaking her head. "I don't know what the hell I'm doing." The tears began welling up, and she couldn't stop them this time.

Bronx put his hand on the back of her head as she laid her forehead on his chest. He kissed the back of her head as she grabbed the sides of his t-shirt. When she finally looked up at him, he drew his head back. "Jorie, what *do* you want?"

What she wanted was to feel bad for her husband, but she really didn't. What she wanted was to stop herself from making love to Bronx again, but she really couldn't. What she wanted was evident minutes later when she was naked in his bed yet again. What she really wanted was for the rest of the world to disappear, and at least in that moment, for the two of them, it did.

Seven

RARELY A DAY PASSED WHEN Jorie went to the apartment to work and they didn't make love. In these stolen moments, it was like every nerve in her body was on fire. She had never been more present in her own reality. At first it was mornings or afternoons when the boys were at school and Grace was at daycare. Eventually it began involving nights when Ryan could be home with the kids. This heightened Jorie's sense of guilt. She knew in her heart she was abandoning her family for 15 minutes of work and two hours of forbidden passion with another man. One night, after Ryan had rushed home from work only to be saddled with three dirty, hungry, screaming kids, Jorie's conscious got the better of her.

"What is there to drink?" she asked Bronx as they lay in his bed.

"I've got water, and maybe some orange juice in the fridge, but I don't know for sure. Do you want me to get you something?"

Jorie pulled the sheet around her as she got out of the bed. "No, I'll look. Got anything stronger?"

Bronx rolled onto his stomach. "I guess. There could be some vodka in the cupboard over the fridge. I haven't looked up there forever."

Jorie went to the kitchen in search of something to 'calm her nerves.' Somewhere in her brain a small voice was telling her that alcohol wasn't the answer to the conflict at hand. Usually she ate when she was stressed, but that was no longer an option.

Jorie found some rum and vodka in the kitchen. Neither looked like they'd been touched in years and were almost full. As she mixed a strong rum and diet coke, she contemplated just what kind of remodeling she would do in the kitchen. Anything to keep her mind off how horrible she felt about herself.

She was on her second drink when Bronx came out of the bedroom. He put one arm around her waist and took the glass with the other hand. He took a drink, kissed her neck, and twisted the cap back on the rum. "Pretty strong," he commented. "You know you can stay over if you want."

There was nothing she would have loved more than to fall asleep in his bed, in his arms. The very thought of crawling into bed next to the man who's heart she was secretly grinding into pieces filled her with such overwhelming dread, she was tempted to have another drink. Then she really would have to stay the night, but she had to go home, and she knew it.

Days passed, then strung together into weeks. Jorie thoroughly enjoyed decorating the loft. Bronx was open to most everything Jorie showed him, but also told her when he didn't like something or if it was too expensive. One evening she brought over a photo of a Kenyon painting to hang over his fireplace.

He looked at it with a blank expression. "It's a square and two circles." She couldn't tell if this was a question or a statement.

"It's not just a 'square and two circles.' It's a Kenyon," she explained. "He's very hot right now. It's supposed to be representative of eternity, being boxed in, redemption, revolution of life."

He said it again, only slower. "It's a square...and two circles."

Jorie smiled and shook her head. "Alright, so no 'deep' art for you. I get it. It's a little more than you budgeted in here anyway."

Bronx looked surprised. "How much is it?"

Jorie flipped the photo over to show him the back where the gallery owner had written the price. He immediately burst out laughing.

She shook her head and turned on her heels. "Alright, Mr. Funnyman. No squares and circles." He was still laughing hysterically when she left the room.

* * * * *

Though she had pledged to avoid the hospital's support group meetings, Jorie still logged on to their website from time to time, checking out the information or looking at new updates. One day a small advertisement at the bottom of the screen caught her eye, and Jorie clicked on it. This led her to another hospital site. It was for a plastic surgeon.

Jorie had contemplated this for some time. She knew that due to years of yo-yo dieting and being obese for so long that it was possible her skin was not going to recover from her weight loss alone. This had been an issue for her the first time she'd slept with Bronx, and though he wasn't bothered by it, she was. Several cute outfits that she'd been tempted to buy were left hanging on the racks in the store because though they fit, they were not flattering. Jorie didn't expect to have the body of a teenager, but she felt like having lost all the weight that she had, it would be nice to see more of the results with her clothes off.

That was the sentiment she conveyed to Ryan when she approached him about it later that evening. Since the first time she'd approached him about having elective surgery, Jorie had gained a certain amount of self-confidence. She reminded him that not only were the kids a little older and able to be more helpful, she was making more money having gone back to work and doing Bronx's loft on the side. Jorie almost choked on the last part, fearing she might leave off the word "loft" inadvertently.

Though Ryan was little more excited about this surgery than he was the first, he'd learned over the past few months it was pointless to argue with his wife when she set her mind to something. He was well aware of the new confidence Jorie sported. Sometimes he found it sexy, other times it was infuriating. Either way, he had no real argument against the procedure. Ryan agreed to let her start with arm surgery, and they could discuss the rest after they knew how the first one went. Jorie was content with that for the time being, and set about to find out the best surgeon in town.

Discussing it with Bronx proved to be more nerve-racking for Jorie than her husband, who was actually going to be involved in paying for it. It bothered her that Bronx's opinion meant more to her than Ryan's, but she wasn't sure how to change that. One afternoon they were lying together on the couch, laughing about some drama going on in Jorie's office, when she brought it up. Bronx stopped laughing, and gave her a disapproving look.

"Do you really want to do that? I think you have a beautiful body."

Jorie looked at him for a moment, contemplating how to say what had been on her mind for weeks. "I know you deal with it, the extra skin, but you can't tell me you like it."

"No, I wouldn't say I like it," he responded honestly, "but I don't think you should have to go through more surgery. I'm not saying you shouldn't do it, do what you want. I'm just giving you my two cents, since you're bringing it up."

Jorie hadn't expected this reaction, and found herself surprisingly irritated by it. She sat up and took a drink from her wine glass on the coffee table. She shook her head. "Really? What a crock of shit!" She was now a few drinks into her afternoon, and didn't feel much like mincing words. "You seriously expect me to believe that, after the way we started?"

Bronx looked at her, confused. "What are you talking about?" he asked, sitting up himself.

She let out a stiff laugh. "I'm talking about the fact that you didn't even give me a second look before I had my first surgery, so don't act now like you are above caring about looks."

Bronx put a hand on her back. "Are you doing this for me?"

"No Mr. Ego, I'm doing it for myself. I'm just surprised that you think I'm really going to believe you would prefer I stay like this," she exclaimed, motioning towards herself. "You're not so holy that I think you had any interest in me before the weight came off."

Now it was Bronx's turn to chuckle. He leaned back on the couch. "Hey, if you want to call me a pig for liking what I like, go ahead. I mean, why did you even have that surgery? So you could play with your kids, feel better, look better? Of course you did. And your attraction to me was what, because I seemed like a really sweet guy? No, at first it was physical; because that's the way it usually happens with people. I could have been a serial killer for all you knew. You don't hear me bitching about it."

"That's your theory, that because I thought you were good looking when I first saw you but you didn't feel the same way until I was thinner, somehow that makes it alright?"

"J, the first time I saw you I wanted you," Bronx told her. "When I left the barbeque that night, I didn't think I was ever going to see you again. It drove me crazy."

She gave him a stony glare. "That wasn't the first time you saw me," she reminded him as she rose from the couch and took a cigarette out to the patio.

Bronx followed her. "Yes, it was." As Jorie began to shake her head in opposition, he continued his explanation. "I know it wasn't the first time I met you. The first time we met you could barely string a sentence together, you ran away and hid in the house, and you're right, I wasn't attracted to you." Jorie looked down at her fingernails, unsure of what was coming next and afraid to look Bronx in the eye. He walked up on her side and slid a hand around her waist. "The first time I *saw* you, really *saw* you at your barbeque, was different. You were funny and sweet and kept saying the wrong things. And you were beautiful. Even when you weren't this thin," he said, squeezing her narrow side. He turned her to face him. "You were beautiful because you acted like you gave a shit. You were social, you had fun. So sue me for being more attracted to this 'you.' But it's not just physical. I bet that's not the only part of you that changed after your surgery."

Jorie contemplated what he said and knew he was right. Before her surgery she had wanted desperately to be unnoticed, and usually she got her wish. And though it had taken quite a while to get used to the attention she received as a thinner person, in her heart she had grown to like it, and almost expect it. At nearly 300 pounds she hoped nobody would look her way in the grocery store, and certainly didn't want anyone glancing in her cart to see the unhealthy food she was buying. But in her size six jeans, she reveled in the flirtatious smiles she received from men as she was standing in line at the bank or the drug store.

Jorie wasn't sure what she disliked more; the fact that she'd been called on her own crap, or that she'd picked yet another fight that she couldn't win. Lately it seemed there was little that didn't make her suspicious. Almost as if reading her mind, Bronx asked, "Why are we even having this fight?"

She looked at his blue eyes, something that never failed to make her forget everything wrong that had ever happened in the world. He was being as honest with her as she could have asked for, but she just wasn't used to it. Before Ryan, most guys bolted at the first sign of her neuroticism. Bronx didn't do that. He had a way of explaining things so that she was forced to recognize that there was no logic in her thinking. He was always real with her, and frankly it drove her little nuts. Dealing in reality was something she usually avoided these days. In fact, it was a trait she had learned young and recently revived to get through her current situation. It was the way things had been in her family growing up, and despite a promise to herself that she would never let it get that way for her, there she was. Just as knee deep in the mendacity as when she was young, only now she should have been old enough to know better.

As childhoods went, it never really occurred to Jorie that hers was much different from the norm. Her parents had fought, sometimes loudly and for hours. But she and her sister Addie had found retreat in their bedroom closet. It was a large walk in, and the girls had used the bottom rods to hang big quilts and create their own indoor tents, complete with comfy pillows to lie on and all their stuffed animals for additional company. When the fights got really bad, Jorie and Addie would usually drag in their favorite blankets and snacks they'd snuck out of the pantry, and chat away for hours about what their families would be like when they grew up.

Just as they were approaching their teenage years, their parents decided to give up on the marriage and divorced. Addie, the elder by one year, seemed relieved. It pained Jorie at the time that her sister could possibly be happy about the breakup of their family. She didn't understand how, even with the constant bickering, this could possibly be for the best.

Both girls lived with their mother, and saw their father religiously every other weekend. Jorie never felt a lack of love from either parent, and was especially close to her dad. He would take them out for supper every time he had visitation with them, though he was often critical of how much Jorie ate. This hadn't bothered her then. She had grown up hearing his complaints about one subject or another, and had become accustomed to sometimes being the center of his attention, even if it was negative.

Jorie, never being one who liked to disappoint anyone, had taken to rarely eating on their weekend outings, opting rather to sit in her room and read or study late into the night. All the while she would nibble on whatever had been an easy snack to grab on her way through the kitchen. This also allowed her to wait up for Addie, who would often sneak out of their bedroom window to meet a boyfriend or smoke pot in the park a couple of blocks from their house. Jorie loved hearing Addie's stories. Though she occasionally longed to be more outgoing like her sister, she was mostly content to sit home alone with her food.

The year Addie left for college was the hardest for Jorie. Her food consumption slowed down some as she started sneaking out of the house more herself. Years later when she "Dr. Phil'd it" (Jorie's description for figuring out her rebellious behavior), she considered that it was probably taking her sister's place in the family, or maybe finding a way to be closer to her. Whatever the reason, Jorie found herself doing less studying, less eating, and less behaving. Earlier that school year, she had begun seriously dating someone for the first time. Her parents seemed relieved that she was going out on the weekends and having a more active social life. They were both dating other people at that time, and Jorie felt pretty sure they were just happy to have her out of their hair.

Once she started college, her stabilized weight became unstable again. The freshman 15 turned into the freshman 30, and it just kept climbing from there. She would try the latest and greatest in diet plans, only to watch the scale creep back up higher than before she started. Sometimes quickly, sometimes slowly, but the numbers always grew in the end.

Food really did become her best friend after her junior year of college. It was a connection to her past, a reminder of the strong bond she felt to her dad, however twisted that bond was around food. Mostly it gave her great comfort, as she could eat in her darkened room, and almost see Addie sitting across from her. Addie, munching on her own snack and stifling a tell-tale giggle that would give away the fact that they weren't asleep, as they should have been. When she ate, it was like her family was still there with her. When she ate, she could forget that they were all gone.

* * * * *

As work on the loft began to wind down, Jorie began to wonder what kinds of excuses she could make to get out of the house. It occurred to her, on rare occasions, that she could break things off with Bronx. The thought would pass quickly. She could no sooner convince herself to stop breathing.

An afternoon event took place that Jorie was sure would take the decision out of her hands. She had arrived at Bronx's apartment an hour before some of the final pieces of new furniture were being delivered. It was a ritual for them, allowing time for their impassioned encounters before the delivery or workmen arrived.

Bronx had finished showering and let the men in with their crates and boxes while Jorie finished up in the bathroom. He unwrapped a painting and squatted down to look at it, trying to remember where Jorie said it was going to hang. "J," he yelled towards his bedroom, "where are we putting this pond painting?"

Jorie walked out through the hallway, drying her hair with a towel. She was smiling at his usual blue-collar references to the fine art and antiques she had been selecting to decorate his home. "I thought we could put it on the wall over the…" It was only by virtue of the fact that she had her head tilted to dry her hair that she noticed Ryan standing by the door.

She knew with everything that had been going on, Ryan could have caught her there all alone measuring for curtains and Jorie would have felt guilty. But wearing the extra clothes she had been keeping at Bronx's place, both of them with wet hair from being newly showered, Jorie felt certain the only thing that would have been worse was Ryan walking in on them actually *having* sex. Jorie could feel Bronx's eyes boring into her, but she didn't dare look over at him. She worried she would give everything away in that one glance. Instead, she broke into the biggest smile she could manage.

"Hey, what are you doing here?" Jorie asked as lightly as she could. Jorie took a couple of steps towards Ryan, gauging his reaction.

Ryan looked from his friend to his wife. His voice was monotone. "I was going by here on my way to get some parts for the shop, and I thought I would see how it was going. Some delivery guys had all the doors propped open, so I let myself in. What's going on around here?" He continued to glance back and forth between them.

Jorie broke into her most casual laugh. "Oh my God," she said waving her hand, "we had a bad experience fixing some paint problems the guys from Bennett's left us." Ryan knew she had many problems with the painters from the local company her firm often hired, and wouldn't be surprised to learn Jorie had to touch up their work. "Thank God I had these extra clothes in my gym bag. I was such a mess!"

"Oh yeah?" Ryan said. He took a couple of steps into the room, looking more relaxed. Jorie just hoped Bronx would be able to follow her lead. The three of them hadn't been alone together since she had first started decorating the apartment, and Jorie had often wondered how Bronx would react around her and Ryan. For that matter, she wasn't sure how she was supposed to act. It was no secret that she wasn't planning on leaving her husband, but that didn't mean she felt at all comfortable acting like Ryan's 'wife' in front of Bronx. It was just another in a string of completely awkward results of the mess Jorie had created in her life with these two men.

Bronx, in an effort to lighten the tension in the room, stepped forward and held out his hand to Ryan. For a split second Jorie was afraid Ryan wouldn't take it, but then realized she was being paranoid. Ryan smiled and shook Bronx's hand, moving all the way into the room and glancing at the new furniture being wheeled in by three of the delivery men. "Wow, you guys have been busy! So this is what's been keeping my wife occupied all those late nights."

Jorie and Bronx both nodded and smiled. At least it didn't feel like a total lie. She had been working hard on getting everything in the loft just right. It felt like she was decorating her own home more so than that of a client. Jorie knew it was the idea that this man for whom she had such overwhelming feelings would be living in this space drove her to do her very best work. She could feel exactly what was supposed to go into this place, and it really required very little effort on her part. It all just came to her. This was especially helpful in freeing up time for her and Bronx to spend together.

"Can you get away?" Ryan asked. At first Jorie thought he was talking to her, but when she looked at him she realized he was looking directly at Bronx. "I was going over to Curty's and I thought you might want to ride along. We're having some issues with a power circuit I wanted to talk to you about."

Bronx nodded. "Sure man, I don't think I need to be here for this?" directing the question at Jorie.

She nodded and waved her hand again. "Go, go. I've got it."

Bronx gave her one last gleaming smile as he walked out the door behind Ryan. Just when Jorie thought she felt as low as she possibly could, she realized there were new depths to be reached. As the work men continued to bring in boxes, Jorie poured herself a glass of wine and wondered what the next bottom would bring.

Eight

ONE NIGHT WHEN RYAN WAS out of town on a fishing trip with some buddies, Jorie arranged for a sitter to spend the night at the house with the kids. It was the first occasion they'd spent the entire night together. Though Jorie didn't feel entirely comfortable with leaving the kids all alone with a teenager for the night, she couldn't pass up the opportunity. After the second time they'd made love, she lay on her side next to Bronx, head propped up on her hand. He looked at her, and her stomach was still filled with the same insane butterflies as the first time he'd walked up her driveway.

"What?" he asked in his deep voice. "What are you thinking, lookin' at me like that?"

Her hazel eyes moved back and forth, unable to decide which of his ice blue eyes to focus on. They were the most amazing color she had ever seen, and she felt if that were all she could look at for the rest of her life, she would die happy.

"This is going to sound totally corny," she said softly. "But have you ever wanted to be so close to somebody you feel like if you could crawl right into their skin it wouldn't be close enough?"

Bronx laughed lightly. "This isn't the part where you tell me you're an alien, is it?"

Jorie shook her head, trying to force a slight smile. She knew he was kidding, and it really did sound insanely mushy, but he had asked her how she was feeling. At the moment, that was the best way to put it into words. She wasn't angry with him for his reaction, but wanted him to know she was serious.

"Hey, I'm sorry. I didn't mean to make fun of you. You know I'm not great with the emotional stuff." Bronx said, lacing his fingers through hers. He looked down at their hands intertwined and nodded. "Yeah, I mean, I know what you're talking about. There are days I don't get to see you when I don't know if I can make it to the next time. I guess that's kind of the same thing."

Jorie knew the feeling exactly, and felt a huge pang of guilt at the position she had put him in. There were days when she didn't want to get out of bed because she knew she wouldn't be seeing him until the next day, or maybe the day after that. A couple of glasses of wine later she felt less on edge, but then spent much of the day sleeping or laying on the deck while the kids played in the yard, wishing she could have just an hour with Bronx. The resentment she felt towards her kids for "forcing" her to be a mom rather than going where she wanted led her to another glass and then another. On these days Jorie usually ordered a pizza for Ryan and the kids and went to bed early with a fake migraine. She was starting to worry Ryan was going to send her in for an MRI. In reality, their days apart couldn't go fast enough for Jorie, and the headaches served another purpose. They were the perfect excuse to put off sex with her husband, something Jorie was having a harder and harder time doing without a good explanation.

Bronx looked back at her. "But then you're here, and I really try to remember every second of it because I know it's going to be over again before I know it." Turning from serious to playful, he quickly flipped Jorie over on her back and was lying on top of her. "But if you want to be closer, I think I could probably help you with that."

She giggled as he began kissing her neck, moving slowly down her breastbone and holding her tightly in his arms. If this was as close as she could get to him, she would take his cue and enjoy every minute of it.

The next morning when the sun began streaming through the huge windows lining the bedroom, Jorie reached across the nightstand for her cell phone. She had wanted to make sure Ryan hadn't sent her a text during the night, something he sometimes did during his rare drunken guy weekends. She pushed the button on the phone to light up the screen and nothing happened. She tried again, and in horror realized the phone was off. It suddenly occurred to her that the battery had died the day before, and when she took it off the charger she must have forgotten to turn it back on. With her hand shaking, Jorie turned the phone on, praying nobody had tried to call her during the night.

Before she could even check her voice mail, the phone began ringing and vibrating in her hands. Jorie saw Ryan's name come up on the caller ID and her stomach fell. She could see there were messages in her voice mail, and knew it was an unlikely coincidence that he just happened to be calling her for the first time as she was turning her phone on. In fact, it was barely six in the morning, and she knew he should be sleeping off the night before. This couldn't be good.

"Jorie!" Ryan yelled into the phone. She held it away from her ear, the piercing scream like a nail in her throbbing head. "Where the fuck are you? What are you doing? You need to get over here now!"

The slight hangover and serious lack of actual sleep were put on the back burner. All of Jorie's nerves were firing as she sat straight up in bed. "What, where are you? What's going on?" she asked, suddenly terrified.

"I'm at St. Keats," Ryan almost yelled back, though she could hear no background noise. "Brennan had to have his appendix out, and nobody could get a hold of you. Where the hell are you?" he asked again, lowering his voice as though somebody on his side of the phone told him to keep it down.

"I'll be right there!" she said, avoiding his question yet again. She jumped out of Bronx's bed and ran into the shower. She knew she had to get to the hospital, but didn't want to show up there with the smell of Bronx still on her. He was still asleep when she threw on her clothes and ran out the door.

All the way to the hospital her body trembled. She didn't know if it was nervousness about the condition of her son, guilt over leaving him with a babysitter and forgetting to turn her phone on, or that she really needed a drink right about now. It was probably all three.

As she raced to the pediatric floor of the hospital where Brennan was recovering from his surgery, Jorie pushed the terror of having to answer Ryan's impending questions out of her head. She felt selfish, fearing for her own discomfort when her son was lying in a hospital bed, not even knowing where his mom was. In truth, worrying about what her husband was going to say was easier for her mind to deal with than how terrible she felt about her parenting, or lack thereof. It seemed there was a time when Jorie really prided herself on being a great mom. Now that time seemed like ages ago.

"How is he?" she asked breathlessly, finding Ryan sitting in a bench in one of the long hallways.

"He's good. It was appendicitis, so they took it out and he'll be home in a couple of days. Jorie, where were you?"

Jorie knew she couldn't put it off forever, but right now she just wanted to see her son. "Can we talk about this later? I really need to see Bren."

Ryan opened the door to their son's room, and Jorie made her way quietly to the bedside. She didn't care if they called it "routine." There was nothing routine about seeing her child, an IV in his arm and as pale as the hospital sheets, lying in the sterile room recovering. Jorie was still shaking, but put on her biggest smile as she took Brennan's hand and kissed him all over his face.

"Hi sweetie, how are you feeling?" she asked as she sat on the side of his bed.

Brennan smiled at the sight of his mom. "Alright. My tummy hurts a little, but they are giving me some medicine so it doesn't hurt so much. Where were you, mommy?"

This was going to be easier to dodge than with Ryan, but Jorie felt even more guilt lying to her son. "Mommy was out for a while, and I'm so, so sorry I wasn't here for your operation. But I heard you're going to be right as rain in a day or two. Good as new! Then we can go home and lie on the couch and have lots of ice cream and popsicles and watch movies." She winked at Brennan, whose face lit up at the mention of ice cream and movies on the couch.

"Mom, can you stay with me for a while?" he pleaded when she tried to stand up.

Jorie squeezed his hand. "Absolutely, buddy. I'm just going to pull up a more comfortable chair, but I will definitely stay with you every minute. Mommy's not going anywhere."

The minutes ticked by into hours, and Jorie didn't move from Brennan's room for anything. She was craving a cigarette, a drink, even a diet soda, but she didn't dare leave the room. In part because she felt so terrible about having been unavailable when her child needed her, and also to avoid being caught alone with Ryan and his inevitable questions about where she had been. As long as she stayed in the room, she was safe. He would never bring it up in front of their son. Fortunately, Ryan was the first to volunteer to run for supplies.

"I think I'll go home and check on Jack and Grace, and get some clean clothes. What do you want me to bring back?" Ryan asked.

Jorie was grateful to have some time alone. Shortly after Ryan left Brennan fell asleep, giving her a chance to duck out and call Bronx, who had already called a couple of times. She felt terrible about the way she'd run out of his place without even waking him to tell him where and why she was going, but he understood. Though she would have given almost anything for him to be able to come up to the hospital and be her support, just talking to him on the phone calmed her nerves a bit.

Over the next couple of days Jorie managed to avoid any time alone with Ryan, thereby putting off the impending discussion of her night away from home. She had wanted to come up with a plausible story, but didn't feel like she could focus on getting a good story together while dealing with Brennan being ill. He recovered quickly though, and when it was time for him to go home Jorie felt the anxiety building within her, knowing the time was coming when she'd have to answer to her husband.

Ryan wasted little time asking the question. As soon as they had all the kids in bed their first night home together from the hospital, he sat on the edge of their bed as she sorted laundry to be washed.

"So, are you ever planning on telling me where you were on Saturday night? It's not like you to leave the kids with Molly and not tell me you're going to be gone overnight. Actually it's not like you to be gone overnight at all."

The tone in Ryan's voice was calm, but Jorie could tell there was enough of an edge to know there was no way to duck out of it this time. She continued sorting, keeping her head down. She had come to the conclusion that the only thing to do was tell the truth. Well, not the truth exactly, but an altered version of the facts.

"This remodel at Bronx's place is taking way longer than I thought. He was going to be out of town visiting some family, so I thought it would be a good time to get some work done over there, and I guess I had too much wine because I fell asleep on the couch. I forgot to turn my phone on after the battery charged and I'm really sorry. I screwed up. I was just trying to get this finished without taking too much more time away from the family." Jorie looked up at him tentatively, reading his reaction to see if he was buying it.

"Why didn't you just tell me this when I first asked?" Ryan asked, seemingly unconvinced.

Jorie was just making things up as she went along now. "Because I knew you'd be pissed that I had too much to drink, and I didn't want to get in a big fight with Brennan in the hospital. Really Ryan, it was an honest mistake. It could have happened to anyone."

Ryan seemed to contemplate what his wife had told him. She couldn't tell if he really believed her version of the events, or if he just really wanted to. "I guess I don't know why you'd be sitting over there drinking wine while you were working?" he questioned, raising an eyebrow.

This was the part of the story where Jorie had to make a sacrifice. She knew that Ryan was not impressed with her drinking lately, but it certainly felt safer to confess to drinking too much rather than having sex with another man. This way she could get into an adequate amount of trouble without having to admit to what she was really doing. Jorie felt like a teenager again, lying to her parents about where she was, but that was the situation she had placed herself in. And now that the story was out, there was no going back.

"I know, it was stupid. I was just stressed from the week and thought since I wasn't with the kids and didn't have to be responsible to anyone for the night that it wouldn't be any big deal. I said I'm sorry, I've told Bren I'm sorry. What else can I do?" Jorie ended her statement with a bit of a whine that told Ryan she was really done discussing it.

Apparently so was he, because he took the remote from the night stand and leaned back on the bed. "OK, alright. Can you please just tell me these things from the beginning so we don't have this kind of issue again?" Ryan looked at Jorie, remote poised in his hand but not turning on the TV until he felt like he had a satisfactory answer from her.

"Yes, sure, again I'm sorry."

Ryan flipped on the TV, apparently resigned to the fact that his wife was probably just a boozer rather than the cheating, lying adulteress she felt like. Since she couldn't or wouldn't undo the latter, she took down a load of the laundry and decided to deal with it in her new 'usual' way. She got drunk.

* * * * *

Try as she might to drag out finalizing the work on Bronx's remodel, the day came when Jorie had to admit she was done. She'd made the work last as long as possible, but in the end she was growing more concerned about Ryan's constant questioning of her progress. Especially in light of the dark cloud still hovering after Brennan's surgery.

The weekend after she finished, Bronx stopped by to help Ryan with a project in the backyard. Jorie was a little rattled to see him at her house, but at the same time elated about the unexpected run-in. She and Gina were sunbathing on the back deck while the kids played in the sprinklers. Jorie inwardly smiled at the thought of being able to lie on the lounge chair, drink her wine and watch Bronx work in the hot sun. She was about to break into full grin at the idea that his shirt might even come off when Gina asked him a question that caught her completely off guard.

"So when are we going to get to see this great loft of yours?"

Jorie almost choked on her drink. "Nice Gina, just invite yourself over."

"No, I'm just saying. You've been working on this for months, and according to you it's your best work. This was a huge deal, Jor." Gina looked up at Bronx over the top of her sunglasses. "We really don't get to see much of Jorie's work because it's usually just for clients from the firm, and it's not usually an entire home. I'm just suggesting a house-warming party. Then I can invite myself to that," she finished with a self-satisfied smile.

Ryan overheard the end of the conversation as he walked up on the deck, messing with a tool in his hand. "A party sounds cool. We'd love to go, right babe?" he said to Jorie.

Jorie opened her mouth, but no sound came out. Bronx broke into a broad grin and came to the rescue.

"Yeah, OK," he started slowly. "I can do that. I don't know anything about having a house-warming party, but it can't be too hard." Bronx looked over at Gina. "You want to do the actual planning part? I'll make sure the place is relatively clean and the door is unlocked."

"Great," Gina said with a slight smirk. If Jorie didn't know better, she'd swear Gina was flirting with Bronx. Right then, all Jorie could think of was having to mingle with friends of Bronx, Ryan and her's at a party in the house where she'd been betraying her family for months. Where her deluded husband would be at her side while she herself was basically the guest of honor. Where she would have to spend the evening politely accepting countless compliments on her work, all the while knowing the scandalous things that had taken place in every room in Bronx's apartment. Jorie wasn't sure she was up to that kind of guise.

"Yeah, great," she sighed, trying to force a smile. Jorie swallowed the rest of the wine in her glass and stood up to get a refill. "Just let me know when."

Thanks to several scheduling conflicts, three weeks passed and Jorie hadn't heard one word about the house-warming party at Bronx's. She was beginning to let herself consider the possibility that they had forgotten about it, but of course that would have been too convenient. If Jorie was learning anything during this affair, it was that rarely was any part of it convenient.

"Jor, I need to know if the 14th is going to work for you, because it's starting to look like the only day this month we're going to be able to do this thing," came Gina's breathless voice on the phone one morning. "Otherwise possibly the 28th, but I really hate to move it back that far. Plus there seems to be a lot going on that weekend and I'd have to probably juggle some things. Oh, and we could probably only get the bartender until nine that night and not sure on the caterer. So, does that work for you?"

"Does what work for me?"

"The 14th!" Gina barked, aggravated.

"Yeah, fine, whatever," sighed Jorie. "Gina, you really don't have to do this. It's not that big of a deal. And what, why are you talking about bartenders and caterers? Did you come into some money all of a sudden?"

"It was so weird. I talked to Bronx the other day, and we were talking about what to do for the party and I mentioned how cool it was that people were going to be able to admire your great work for a change. He just sort of changed from uninterested to asking me how much money I needed to make it a big deal. Well I didn't really know, and I didn't want to tap the guy if he couldn't afford it, but it turns out he really can. What's the deal with that? Isn't he, like a plumber or something?"

"An electrician," Jorie corrected. She was barely listening anymore. Her head shook in disbelief. He wanted the party to be special because it was for her. He didn't care about showing his house off to anyone. This was about Jorie.

"OK, so do they make bank because he's really going all out for this thing?"

Jorie snapped back to the conversation at hand. "Well, I think he has some money from his family. His father. That's where he got the loft in the first place. His dad left it to him when he died. He spent a few bucks on the remodel. But this is crazy. He doesn't need to throw money away on a party."

Gina chuckled. "Hey, go ahead and try to talk him out of it. I think he's more into this planning thing than I am at this point. I doubt you're going to change his mind. Anyway, if he didn't already have a girlfriend I'd swear he has a little crush on you."

"Wait, what? He has a girlfriend?" Jorie wasn't sure she'd heard that right.

"Didn't you know that? You practically lived over there. You mean you've never met her?" Gina questioned skeptically.

Jorie tried to organize her thoughts, but it came out all jumbled. "Yeah, well I guess, yeah, he did mention something about some girl. I don't know…for sure. I didn't ask a lot of questions. I was his decorator, not his social director," Jorie finished, a little more harshly than she intended.

Gina didn't seem to notice. She was off again on party planning mode. "Well, I guess she's traveling and won't be around no matter what day we have the party. Sucks either way for me. He's seriously hot. So I don't remember if you answered my question. Is the 14th alright or what?"

Jorie assured her it was fine, both women in a hurry to get off the phone. Gina had more party plans to work on, and Jorie had a phone call of her own to make.

Two minutes later she reached Bronx on his cell phone. Despite the background noise Jorie heard from where he was working, she didn't feel bad about bothering him. She was curious to know just what Gina was talking about, and Jorie didn't think she could wait until the next time they were getting together.

"Hey," Bronx said quietly. "What's going on?"

Jorie tried to keep her tone light. She didn't want to sound like a jealous lunatic. "Hey yourself. I was calling to ask you the same thing. I just got off the phone with your very efficient party planner and she had some interesting things to say." The noise on Bronx's phone was starting to annoy her. "Where are you anyway?"

"I'm working, at a shop over on Porter," he said pointedly.

"You're at Ryan's shop?"

"Yeah. Sorry about the noise. What were you saying about the party?" The background noise on Bronx's phone went from industrial to nature, and Jorie figured he had moved outside for some quiet.

"Well," she began, "I was just a little curious about the party, and why you're spending all this money?" Jorie paused. "Oh yeah, and about your girlfriend. The one Gina thinks you have? I was wondering when I was going to get to meet her?"

Bronx laughed. "I'm thinking you want to know the answer to the last question first. Gina was pretty sure I needed a date for this thing, and I wasn't sure how to get around that so I guess I just said the first thing that came to mind. And about the party. I don't know. I just want to do something special for you. I mean, we're...us together, that's incredible. But what you did to my place is awesome. I just think you deserve something awesome too."

Jorie blushed at the suspicious way she had questioned him. Could she have really done that, questioned the loyalty of the man with whom *she* was having an affair? With the phone cradled on her shoulder, she opened the pantry door. Nothing looked good. Then she went to the fridge and found the half a bottle of wine she had opened the night before. An hour later she barely recalled what her original problem had been, let alone the embarrassment of her reaction to it.

Nine

THE NIGHT OF THE PARTY arrived, and the passage of time had done little to reduce Jorie's apprehension about the event. If anything, the longer she had to wait the more the dread built in her. When Ryan tried to take her hand as they walked into Bronx's building Jorie jumped as though she'd been electrocuted. He put his hand on her back.

"Hey, what's wrong? This is going to be fun," he assured her.

Jorie wanted to tell her husband that if he put his hand on her again she was going to come right out of her skin. Her irritation with him was pretty much constant these days, but being in Bronx's place heightened the feeling. She wanted to feel guilty about it, but that emotion had long since been so buried that Jorie didn't even know where she could find it anymore.

Gina was in her element. Jorie's anxiety was eased some by seeing her best friend so ecstatic to be involved in arranging the party and making every detail perfect. She had managed to arrange everything for the party without taking away from any of the decorative work Jorie had done on the loft.

"This place is just amazing Jor," Gina gushed. It wasn't like her to be overly sentimental, but Jorie could tell that Gina was taken aback by how the remodel had come out.

"Thanks," Jorie blushed. "It really wasn't all me though. The space was so cool to work in. I just let it inspire me."

"It really is inspired," came Bronx's deep voice from behind Jorie and Ryan. She just glanced at him, floored by how incredible he looked in his black dress pants and shirt. Sometimes for Jorie looking at him was like looking directly at the sun.

Ryan shook his head and motioned around the room with a beer in his hand. "It's just great, honey," he said, then gave her a kiss on the cheek.

"Well come on," Gina coaxed. "I need the official decorator's tour so I know what everything is." Jorie spent the next hour greeting people, fielding a stream of compliments and explaining all the details of the work she'd done in the loft.

She was thrilled to see several of her friends, but even more intrigued to meet Bronx's. Though she knew it was because of her that their relationship was so covert, it hadn't occurred to her just how much of his life she didn't know. Jorie was disheartened by this thought. She watched him from across the room, laughing with a neighbor she'd seen coming and going but had never met. Her brain felt like it was swimming in her skull, and she literally had to lean on the wall she was standing by to keep from falling over. Jorie wasn't sure how much longer she was going to be able to keep up with her double life. More and more lately she had been considering that even though she'd sworn to Ryan they would never put their kids through it, the time may have come to think about a divorce. Jorie just didn't know how she was going to go home that night with her husband, leaving behind the man to whom she was so addicted.

Just as Jorie turned to Ryan to tell him they needed to talk, he squeezed her arm and moved to an open spot next to the bar. Before Jorie knew what was happening, Ryan had loudly asked for everyone's attention.

"Hi, everyone. Thanks so much to all of you for coming tonight. I know it means the world to Jorie, after all the work she put in here.

As you can see, it was well worth the time. She did an incredible job. And thanks to Gina and Bronx for putting this party together." Ryan looked distinctly at Bronx. "I just want to let you know I'm taking my wife back, man." Jorie's pulse promptly stopped. Then Ryan broke into a huge grin. "You've hogged her long enough! I know her kids want her back, and so does her husband." Ryan looked devotedly at his wife. It took a second for Jorie to realize all eyes in the room were on her. Cue fake smile.

"Jorie," he continued. "I suggested this job to you because I know how hard you worked making our house into a home. I thought Bronx deserved that too, and you did not disappoint. I love you," he said, raising his beer bottle in a toast.

Everyone else raised their drinks as well-- ooh's and ah's coming from the crowd in response to Ryan's kind words. Jorie, face still adorned with her best fake happiness, couldn't resist glancing at Bronx. He had his bottle in the air, but as he tipped it back to drink to her with the rest of the guests, Jorie thought she saw something else behind his radiant white smile. It was pain. He nodded at her, then turned and disappeared behind the people coming up to congratulate Jorie.

She shook hands and exchanged cheek kisses with several people as quickly as she could. Once Ryan reached her, she planted the slightest of pecks on his lips. "Thank you, honey," she said, trying not to sound as forced as it felt. "I'm just going to check on everything at home." Jorie held up her cell phone and a pack of cigarettes. "I'll be back."

Ryan nodded, a look of satisfaction on his face. He was not big on speaking in front of people, and seemed relieved to be left to huddle with a couple of guys from work who Jorie still couldn't believe had actually come to a house-warming party.

Jorie felt like a thief, stealing her way to the back of the apartment, glancing behind her to make sure nobody noticed her movements. She slunk into Bronx's bedroom, and noticed the light on under the bathroom door. Jorie glanced around one more time to be sure nobody else was around. She knocked gently on the door.

It opened almost immediately, and Bronx looked at her, his silver-blue eyes dancing.

"I'm sorry," she almost whispered.

Bronx shook his head. "You don't have to be. He's your husband, and he loves you."

Jorie pushed her way past him and closed the door. "What are you doing?" he asked. Jorie set her wine glass on the counter and stood in front of Bronx. She reached for the belt around his waist and began to undo it.

Bronx put his hands on her arms, stifling a laugh. "J, you know we can't do this now."

"No I don't," she smiled slyly as she finished unbuckling his belt and proceeded to undo his button and zipper.

Now Bronx laughed right out loud. "Jorie, there are a lot of people out there who came to see either you or me. One of us should probably be out there."

Jorie shook her head. She reached down the front of Bronx well-pressed black dress pants. "I don't want to talk to them now. I don't want to talk at all." Bronx's entire body tensed as the impact of her touch hit him. He moved as though to try one more time to stop her, but he couldn't. He spun the two of them around, pulling off her underwear from beneath her dress and lifting her up onto the marble countertop in one quick motion. Jorie pushed his clothing out of the way and pulled him inside her. As their lips touched, she felt tears welling behind her eyes. In just a few thoughtful words Ryan had managed to defeat any nerve she had built up to tell him the truth about their marriage, and Bronx. Jorie buried her face in Bronx's neck, willing away the trapped feeling she'd been carrying around so long.

* * * * *

Ryan came in with a little extra bounce from work. He walked up to Jorie as she was standing in front of the sink washing her hands, and put his arms around her waist. If he noticed her tense up when he did this, he didn't mention it.

"Hey, how was your day?" He leaned around to give her a kiss, but she extended her cheek to make sure that's where it landed.

"Alright," Jorie said, trying to sound upbeat. She reached for a towel to dry her hands, making every effort to avoid eye contact with her husband. "How about yours?"

Ryan began sorting through the mail he had brought in with him, then paused and looked at Jorie. "It was good. I have a little surprise for you."

Jorie looked at him, wondering what it could be. Was there a chance Ryan had another woman in his life? Had he decided to move on? Nope, too easy.

"If you think you can get a sitter together in the next hour, we're going out with some guys from work." There was an excitement in his voice Jorie rarely heard, especially these days. "Chuck and some of the guys put together a night out where we can actually bring our wives." Seeing she was less than enthused, Ryan's tone took a slight downturn. "What, I thought you'd love this? You're always saying we never go anywhere together. We never get to do anything with other couples. You're never here anymore…" His voice trailed off as she guessed he was approaching an irritated tone and didn't want to start a fight.

"I know, I know. It sounds like fun." She tried with all her might to put even the slightest hint of excitement in her voice.

As though there was never any tension in the room, Ryan's mood instantly lifted and he smiled at his wife. "Good, because I want to show off my beautiful new wife." As he said this, he walked up in front of her and put his arms around her waist once more. They went much further now than they had months earlier. Jorie put the flats of her hands on his upper arms to offer resistance.

"I've been your wife for 12 years," she said, irritated. "I'm not new."

Ryan looked hurt as he backed away. "You know what I meant," he began. But it was too late. The mood in the room changed. "So are we going?" he asked her, pleading with his eyes.

"Yeah, we'll go. Let me call Molly and see if she can come over." Jorie walked over to the phone, hoping Ryan would let things go from that point. She didn't feel like getting into any deep conversations right now. What she felt like was a drink, and the more she thought about it, the more appealing this night out sounded. Even if it was with her husband.

Ninety minutes later, the kids were fed, babysitter in place, and Jorie was dressed in one of her favorite new outfits. Going out with Ryan's co-workers was not something they did very often, and some of them had not seen her since before the weight loss. She was excited to see people who had only seen her heavy, mostly because the looks on their faces were priceless. Most tried to either be overly congratulatory, or act like they hadn't really noticed. Like she had looked like that to them all along. But every once in a while she'd run into somebody who was blown away and had to bring it up right away.

No matter what the reactions she was going to be getting tonight, it was nothing compared to the reaction she had to Ryan's announcement in the car.

"So remember the other week when we were discussing Bronx maybe having a girlfriend? How he never wanted to get together with us as a couple and I couldn't figure it out. He would come over for a beer or to barbeque, but not anything else?" Jorie instantly felt her stomach drop to the very lowest point in her body. Her ears became red and the bottoms of her feet were tingling. She knew this was the discussion she had been dreading for months.

"Yeah?" she managed, almost inaudibly.

"That son-of-a-bitch is finally bringing her out so we can actually meet her."

"WHAT?" Jorie almost screamed, turning to look at Ryan as though he had just informed her that why of course aliens are real dear, and not only was he one of them but he was their leader, sent down to have her spawn an entirely new race of mutant human aliens.

"I know. Crazy, huh?" Ryan said, laughing and shaking his head.

Jorie felt her breathing becoming heavier, and a buzz started in her head so loud she couldn't make out the rest of what Ryan was saying. Something about Bronx maybe finally being ready to settle down, he wondered what she was like, was glad his buddy wasn't turning out to be gay, not that there would be anything wrong with it if he was…

She didn't really care what Ryan thought about the situation. She reached for a cigarette and cracked the window. It was rare for her to smoke with anyone else in the car, but this was one time she was just going to have to make an exception. Jorie didn't know if it was the excitement of finally meeting this "mystery woman" or that Ryan didn't want a repeat of their earlier tension, but he didn't say a word. He just rambled on about how he was as shocked as she was when Bronx called, blah, blah, blah.

"I wish you would have mentioned this to me earlier," Jorie blurted out, even surprising herself with the venomous tone in her voice. She hadn't meant to be so obvious in her anger, but couldn't seem to think straight enough to hide her feelings at this point.

"Geez Jor, I didn't think it was going to piss you off. I thought you'd get a kick out of it. It's just dinner for Christ sakes. What is going on with you tonight?"

Jorie shook her head as she turned towards the cracked window and blew smoke out, hoping her frustration would go right along with it. She knew this feeling wasn't going away, but getting into a battle with Ryan over it in the car was just going to make things worse. Let's see, how could she explain how inconsiderate it was of him to not mention that the man she had been having an affair with was bringing another woman to dinner? Hmmm, that was a tough one to tackle right at that moment. Maybe another course of conversation?

"You know, this was a really long week. I don't know what my problem is right now. Sorry. You're right," she turned from his curious gaze to look back out her own window, "it's really crazy." He didn't notice the sarcasm in her voice, much as he hadn't noticed a lot of things about her these days.

When they pulled up outside the restaurant, Jorie thought she was going to be sick. There had been barbeques and group functions where she and Bronx had to play the roles of buddy and wife-of-buddy. But tonight was different. Tonight was with Ryan's co-workers, their wives, and most importantly some other woman who would be playing the role of Bronx's love interest.

Actually, Jorie felt the term woman might have been just a little strong for this particular player in their interesting little game. When they approached the table, Jorie's eyes went automatically to the one person at the table she had never seen before. *I hope they carded her before they brought her that drink*, was the first thought that popped into her head. Next to Bronx sat a girl, who looked barely old enough to drink, with long blonde hair, huge green eyes and a skin-tight pink halter dress. Jorie wanted to think it was sleazy, but the truthfully she knew that it was actually pretty flattering on the young woman. That's it, that's what she was; a fit, smiling, bouncing young woman.

"Hey, there he is!" Ryan beamed. Jorie actually felt herself rolling her eyes at Ryan's enthusiasm before she could stop. Bronx was shaking Ryan's hand and either didn't notice or didn't let on. Jorie did her best to paste on that plastic smile she'd been carrying around with her for so many months. This was going to be the performance of a lifetime if it killed her. There had been too many close calls where her reactions and behavior where Bronx was concerned should have been a huge blinking Vegas-type sign telling her husband exactly what had been going on. Whether he was truly oblivious or just in denial she didn't know, and didn't want to risk rocking the boat right then, in front of all these people and the new "girlfriend." Jorie put her hands at a respectable height on Bronx's arms and leaned in for the obligatory cheek kiss before being introduced to his lovely dinner date, Ainsley. Jorie bit her tongue to keep from asking her what kind of dumbass name that was and what kind of drugs her parents had been abusing when they gave it to her. The truth was Jorie thought it was a pretty name, and thought it suited the young woman quite well. Man, this sucked!

Ryan acted as though he was meeting his own son's new wife for the first time. Jorie couldn't tell if it was Ainsley's attractiveness or just the idea that his friend was finally out with this mystery woman that was causing her husband to act so giddy. Maybe he really did suspect what had been going on between his Bronx and Jorie, and felt this was an indication he was wrong. Whatever it was, Ryan's behavior was causing her to want to ask him for a divorce right there at the table. As though he wasn't on her nerves enough lately…

Jorie shook Ainsley's hand and told her how nice it was to meet her, finally. She then promptly turned on her heels and ordered a double rum and coke from the server who was approaching the table. He informed her that he wasn't their waiter and that one should be by shortly. Jorie shook her head at him as he tried to explain this. She leaned in so that only he would hear her and held out a $20 bill.

"No, you don't understand. I *really* need a drink right away." Jorie's eyes got bigger the more she spoke. "I'm sure our server is on her way, but since you're already here can you please just bring it for me?"

The server looked at the bill, took it from her hand with one quick swoop and smiled at her knowingly. "Yes ma'm, I can do that." She patted his arm as a thank you and now hurry along gesture. She then turned back to the group of people seated at the long table. This was going to be a long night.

Jorie hadn't wanted to be social before having a drink or two, but it was too late for that. Several of Ryan's coworkers and their wives were mingling and wandered over to say hello. She fielded the standard compliments and questions about her surgery, grateful for the distraction from the situation on the other side of the table and irritated at the same time that she couldn't keep an eye on the whole thing.

From time to time Jorie heard Ainsley laughing and noticed her touch Bronx's hand gently or lean in to whisper something to him. She would nod and smile at questions from the other men who had approached them from the group, and link her arm with Bronx's as though she was afraid of losing him. Jorie noticed him trying to catch her eye a couple of times. He even smiled and raised his drink towards her once when it didn't seem like anyone around either of them was paying attention. She was all for keeping up appearances, but there was no way she was playing this little game if the cameras weren't rolling. His smile disappeared when he realized she wasn't amused with this charade, and a hurt look crossed his handsome face. God she wanted to kiss him, but she wanted to kill him at the same time.

The waitress took their order, and Jorie (already on her fourth drink) asked for a small salad. She didn't feel like eating anything, but she figured she should have something in her stomach before the alcohol made her sick. And this was dinner out. She could hardly be the lush who sat there all night ordering drinks and not eating any food. How would that look?

Ryan ate with more vigor than he usually had, and even made a toast during dinner to "new friends" and some other nonsense. Jorie wanted to throw her glass at him, but thought it would be a waste of a perfectly good drink.

Before most of their group was done eating, Jorie felt full and really felt she needed a cigarette. She quietly asked the server where smoking was allowed, as she had noticed a sign on the front door barring it within 30 feet of the building. The waitress whispered to her there was a secluded spot behind a wooden fence just off the patio in the back which the staff used, but she didn't hear it from her. Jorie politely excused herself from the table, taking extra care to not make eye contact with Bronx.

The first drag gave Jorie that relaxing sensation she had been craving all evening. She put her head back against the wooden fence that extended high above her, blocking any view of the restaurant or surrounding buildings. How did she manage to get herself into this situation? This thought crossed her mind many times a day in recent months, but it had never been screamed at her quite as loudly as tonight.

"Are you gonna share that?" came the sultry voice that made her stomach fall into her arches, even when she was as mad as she was at that moment. Her finger tips tingled, as did so many other parts of her body. The conflicting feelings hit her as hard as the last drink she had, which might have been number six or seven. She'd lost count. Jorie burst into tears.

Bronx instantly pulled her to him and held her tightly. "Hey, what is it baby?" She wanted to hug him back, but the image of his "girlfriend" laughing, touching his arm, whispering in his ear reminded her of the anger that had been seething in her all night. She pushed him away as hard as she could, almost sending him right to the ground.

"Get away from me!" Jorie tried to keep her voice down so they wouldn't call attention to the fact that they were both back there. Even in her half-drunken state she was so rehearsed at hiding their relationship she could manage that.

Bronx looked like he was bordering somewhere between mild amusement and exhausted frustration. As he noticed the serious-ness on Jorie's face his mood leaned towards the later. He tried to keep it light though as he chuckled and asked her, truly wanting to know, "What the hell? Are you really pissed?"

"Am I pissed, are you serious? How could you bring that woman, or I should say 'girl' here? Who is this person? Why would you do this?" Jorie's hurt was becoming obvious in her voice, but she tried to push it back. She wanted to be mad but had never been very good at combining the two.

Bronx got the biggest smile on his face, and for a moment she thought she was seeing things. It was the most handsome, sexy smile she had ever seen, and the conflicting feelings that had driven her crazy all night were in overdrive now. He shook his head gently, the disbelief oozing from every word.

"Holy shit, you are mad, and you're *jealous*. I can't believe it." Bronx looked her squarely in the eyes as he leaned towards her, the smile immediately disappearing from his chiseled face. "You TOLD me to do this. You said I had to do something so that your husband wouldn't keep wondering why he never got to meet this mystery woman in my life. Does any of that ring a bell with you? Do you recall that little conversation, because I believe you were almost as drunk as you are now, insisting that I introduce Ryan to somebody, anybody else who could throw him off?"

Jorie stopped the drink half-way to her lips, as the hazy wine-soaked memory of what Bronx was talking about came into focus. She was sure that Ryan was on to them. He had been going on for days about how odd it was that Bronx never brought his girl over for any parties or out to any work events. Ryan said maybe she was married, and looked so pointedly at Jorie she felt like he was boring a laser beam into her head. She laughed at Ryan and said "Yeah, maybe. Wouldn't that be crazy?" The very next time she and Bronx were together she did tell him about the conversation with her husband. She had asked him to fix it, and apparently he thought he was. But she still didn't understand something.

"Fine, so I told you to. But what, did you have instant girlfriend-in-a-can just sitting around waiting to meet your friends like you've been together forever? How long have you been dating her?" Yeah, that's what she was going to be mad about now. No sense in quitting while she was behind.

"I'm not dating her," Bronx said softly as a slight smile returned to his face. "She goes to college with my nephew Alex. They're in the drama department together. I helped them move some props for a show the day after you insisted I get a flesh-and-blood girlfriend, and we started talking about it. He has a huge crush on her, which is kind of weird because I always thought the kid was gay..."

Jorie held up the hand with a newly-lit cigarette. "Point, please."

"Yeah, so anyway I was joking with Alex about it, and I guess he thought this would be a good way for him to spend more time with her. He brought her over to my place a couple of times so we could get our stories straight, and then when Chuck set this up today I happened to be doing some work at the shop and so he invited me. It seemed as good a place as any to bring her, so I did. I tried to call you about it earlier, but you didn't answer and I didn't dare leave a message. This is what you said you wanted J. And everyone seems be going for it. She's a pretty good actress, huh?" He had a look of satisfaction on his face, though a hint of guilt showing through. It endeared him to her even more. He had done this for her, to save her marriage to another man when all he ever wanted to was to have her all to himself.

"You're really not sleeping with her?" Jorie felt stupid, angry with herself, and drunk.

Bronx shook his head as he reached for her smoke, took a drag, then reached for her glass. "Nope, feel free to ask her. Or better yet, you can come with me to the play they're doing next week at the college. The lighting is great. I should know; that's what I got to do as payment for her little performance here tonight." Bronx chuckled; obviously amused with his method of payment being electrical work for a play, or maybe it was disbelief that he had come to this point himself. He raised the glass to his lips, took a sip, and screwed up his face.

"Geez Jorie, is there any soda in here or is it straight?" He had never known her to be a straight liquor drinker. She had asked for a mixed drink, but asked that it be a short double, with a little extra. Maybe that didn't make it much of a mixed drink anymore. She hadn't really thought much of it.

Jorie put her arms around Bronx's neck and drew him in for a slow, deep kiss. He was stiff at first, still incensed by her tantrum. It only lasted a moment. Drunk, angry, spiting fire, it didn't matter to Bronx. He had no ability to reason when she was around. Logic played no part in anything they had to do with each other. He was just a guy who had never even considered intentionally misleading anyone, yet on this night he'd spent the whole evening convincing his friends and co-workers that he was dating some 22-year old acting student he barely knew. It was like something out of a bad romance novel; only Bronx didn't figure you could make this stuff up.

All the muscles in his body relaxed as he leaned her onto the fence blocking them from view. His arms wrapped around her back, then his hands went to waist, to her hips. He dropped his kiss to her neck. She moaned as her head went back and one leg wrapped around his calf. Countless times in his embrace and she could barely remember a time she wanted to make love to him more intensely than she did then.

Bronx raised his lips to her ear, his breath hot and quick. "I love you." He softly kissed her one more time and then ducked out of the opening in the fence. It was the first time he had said it, but Jorie knew. Everything he had done for her, to preserve her family, to honor her wishes had told her that, and she knew.

Ten

THE WORDS STUCK WITH JORIE for days. She mulled them over, contemplated them, cherished them, loathed them. The conflict of emotions confused her. Why would she not want to hear that? What was it about being loved that scared the shit out of her and made her feel so incredible at the same time? Part of the problem was that Jorie had not said it back. That night at the restaurant, Bronx had run off so quickly she'd had no chance to respond. But days had gone by, and even though he now told her every time they were together, she hadn't said it to him. Bronx didn't push her, didn't even pause as though he was waiting to see what she'd say. He just said it because he meant it, and that was enough for him. Jorie didn't know if it was enough for her.

"I just don't get what the big deal is? Why do you care either way?" she asked in a huff one night. Ryan had taken the kids to the movies, and she was supposed to be out of town for the evening with some girlfriends. Ever since finishing up the decorating job at Bronx's apartment, she had developed more new "girlfriends" than she could count. She was just relieved that Ryan never asked to meet them, or questioned her much about where they were going. She had a couple who she even said were trying to get pregnant and didn't drink, so she always had a sober ride home. This seemed to appease him just enough that he rarely solicited any more information.

"It's not a big deal at all, J," Bronx said calmly. They had gone to an art gallery; one Jorie had never been to in a neighboring town, which he had asked to see with her. Art was not his thing and Jorie knew it, but since seeing the transformation of his home and watching her work, he tried to show more interest in the things she loved. With one hand on the steering wheel, he reached over and put his hand on her knee with the other. "You asked for my opinion and I gave it to you. It's just a painting. You said you didn't even like it."

Jorie moved her leg towards the door, shaking off his touch. "Just because I didn't like it doesn't mean it wasn't good!"

She knew she was picking a fight. The hors d'oerves at the opening had been too tempting and she felt stuffed. According to her friend Jess, the gallery owner, the caterer had screwed up the wine order, so Jorie only had two glasses. She was in a mood.

As Bronx turned the car into his underground parking garage, Jorie lit a cigarette. Even though he was alright with it, she knew it bugged him just a little when she smoked in his car. She dug her keys out of her purse, and when he stopped, she slammed the door as she got out.

"Where are you going?" Bronx asked, standing by the driver's door.

Jorie climbed into her car, parked in the next space over. "I need to go!" she shouted before closing her car door. She wasn't kidding. Suddenly she felt like she really had to get out of there.

Bronx looked confused. "J, seriously? What the hell are you doing? You can't really be this mad over a painting?" But he may as well have been talking to himself. She quickly backed out as he tried to walk up to the passenger side window.

"I just have to get out for a while!" she yelled again as she rolled down the window. He tried one last time to call her back, but she tore out of the parking structure and was gone. In her rear-view mirror she could see him, standing with one hand on his hip, one arm outstretched and shaking his head.

She didn't know where she was going exactly. She couldn't go home, not that she wanted to. Ryan wasn't expecting her until the next day. He knew she was going to the gallery opening, and was the one who suggested she get a hotel room there instead of driving home after what he was certain would be a night of heavy drinking. It seemed none of her almost pregnant imaginary friends could make it that night.

Jorie drove to an area of town known as The Link. She'd remembered partying there in college, but hadn't been down there in years. Gone were the small eateries and neighborhood bars she had gone to. They had been replaced by huge clubs, flashing lights and mobs of college kids. Oh well, she thought. At that point she wasn't picky about the atmosphere. She just needed a drink.

As soon as Jorie was through the doors she scanned the place for the bar. She made a beeline for a small opening in the crowd along the nearest one and held out a $20 bill. That usually seemed to get the bartender's attention a little faster.

Jorie placed her order, or actually yelled it over the deafening crowd, and turned to see who there was to see. She glanced at the young girl standing next to her and recognized the face.

"Emma?" she asked, squinting in the haze of the strobe lights through the smoke machine cloud coming off the nearby stage.

The girl looked confused. Then her eyes grew huge as she realized who was standing next to her. "Mrs. Asher? Wow, I would have never recognized you!"

Jorie cringed at the name. "Please, just Jorie is fine. How have you been? I can't believe you're even old enough to be in the bar!" Jorie blurted before she even realized it was coming out.

"Oh yeah, for a little while now," Emma laughed. "Things are good. I just started grad school. How about you? How are your kids?"

The last thing she wanted to talk about right then was her family. "They're fine," Jorie said generically.

Emma didn't notice the flat tone in her voice. She glanced around as she picked up her drink. "Who are you here with?"

Jorie's face flushed as she took a long sip of her own drink. "Um, it's just me. Long story."

"Well hey, come hang with us," Emma coaxed. Jorie looked unsure. "Oh come on, it would be totally cool. You don't want to hang out by the bar all alone. Trust me, the players will be all over you."

Jorie smiled in spite of herself, imagining the young men Emma referred to hitting on her, married, mother of three, probably 10 years older than almost anyone in the bar. She nodded appreciatively, grabbed her own drink and followed Emma out the side door onto the deck. There they approached a table full of college-aged kids.

"Hey guys," Emma began as they group quieted and looked in their direction, "this is Mrs., er, Jorie."

Everyone in the group nodded a hello and returned to their previous conversations or whatever was currently more fascinating on their cell phones. Jorie sat next to Emma as her eyes darted around at the other people at the table. All she could think was, what in the hell was she doing there?

"Jorie used to babysit for me, and when I got older I babysat for her kids," Emma explained to a couple of the young women sitting near them.

Jorie blushed. "We don't have to tell them I'm that old, do we?" She tried to sound light, but she was becoming more and more uncomfortable. Emma's friends just laughed as they introduced themselves. She relaxed a little, realizing they didn't seem to care how old she was. As long as their drinks kept coming and their phones kept working, they were happy.

As she put a cigarette to her lips, a flame appeared in front of her. She leaned forward to light her cigarette, then looked up to find out who the hand belonged to holding it. Next to her stood a tall, blonde young man. When she saw his build, all she could think was football player. The word player stuck in her head, like a flashback to when Emma said it at the bar, and she smiled.

"Thank you," she said, nodding her head.

He nodded back, once. "Sure."

Emma motioned towards the young man. "Brady, this is Jorie. Jorie, Brady."

Jorie smiled at Brady, who now held out his hand. As she shook it, she blushed for a second time that night. He looked at her so intently it made her self-conscious. At the same time, she realized she was starting to feel hot all over and her hands were tingling. It had been quite a while since she had somebody his age flirt with her. Jorie didn't even think it had happened when *she* was that age. Not with anybody that looked like Brady.

"Wait!" Jorie said suddenly, narrowing her eyes and cocking her head to the side as she stood up. "You're Brady Jones. I saw you play football last year for UC. You're really good." Jorie couldn't name another player from any other college sports team, but Ryan had made such a big deal about what a great talent the university had in Brady Jones, they had even gone to a couple of games to watch him. Ryan was right. He was definitely headed for the NFL.

"Thanks," Brady said confidently, obviously used to hearing that from many people. "Do you go to UC?"

Jorie rolled her eyes as she broke into a huge grin. "Uh no," she shook her head, "my college days were over a while ago." She couldn't tell if he was trying to flatter her or if he really thought she might be a student. Either way, she would take the compliment.

"Do you need another drink?" he asked, motioning towards her empty glass. Before she could answer, he waved over a nearby waitress who almost appeared to be waiting just on him to place an order. He raised his eyebrows at Jorie as if to ask what she wanted. She found the expression on his face very sexy and told him what she was drinking. He held up two fingers at the waitress, who smiled, nodded and spun on her heals to go get the drinks from the bar.

"Are people always at your beck and call like that?" Jorie wondered out loud, almost regretting the words as they left her lips. She thought it sounded bitchy, but Brady looked amused.

"Yeah, kind of," he smiled. "So you don't go to the U. What do you do?"

She wasn't used to somebody asking about her, other than other moms at her playgroup or people Ryan worked with. Jorie usually started the answer to this question talking about her three kids. She froze for a second. That was not the discussion she wanted to have with this very attractive young man who had focused all his attention on her. She thought quickly.

"I'm a decorator," Jorie answered, taking a drink while hoping the gesture would signal an end to this particular line of questioning. She didn't get her wish, but Brady continued on the conversation in the direction she was going.

"That's cool. So what kind of decorating do you do?"

Jorie could tell that he wasn't really all that interested in her answer. He was making small talk, coming on to her, keeping their attention on each other. Although she knew from Ryan's affinity for local football that Brady wouldn't have any trouble getting the attention of any other girl in the bar. He was good looking and incredible on the field. A thought passed through Jorie's mind, and she suddenly wondered if he was just as good off of it.

* * * * *

A strip of sun shone through the window, just hitting Jorie in her left eye and causing her to keep it shut as she struggled to see her surroundings out of just her right. The pounding in her head didn't help either. She began to lean up on an elbow, trying to adjust her vision to the otherwise dark room. She could make out a desk with a computer on it, a partially opened closet door and various outlines of things hung on the wall. Her head was slow to clear, but within seconds she realized she had no clothes on under the striped sheet that was covering her.

Nobody was else was in the room, but she could tell it was a male's bedroom. Swinging her legs over the edge of the bed caused another fierce pain in her temple. Jorie spotted her clothes on the floor right next to the bed. As she scrambled to put them on, her purse caught her eye, perched on the edge of the computer desk. God please let my phone be in there, she thought.

Jorie had to wait until she was in the hallway where there was enough light to check the contents of her purse. Luckily her phone was there, along with her wallet and what little cash she had left after her night of buying rounds at the bar. As she crept down the stairs towards what she could only hope would be the front door, Jorie got a better look at her whereabouts. As far as she could tell, it was a frat house.

"Jesus Christ," she muttered to herself as she took one last glance around and quietly stepped out into the lucid morning.

The intense early sunshine served as another reminder that her drinking the night before had been more than excessive. Jorie dug her sunglasses out, cursing the warm rays that doused her face. As she walked to the nearest corner, she called Bronx.

"Where are you?" he asked tolerantly. Jorie had to look up at the street signs. She didn't even know. "I'll be there in 15 minutes."

The ride, from where he picked her up to where she'd left her car parked near the bars on The Link, was silent. Jorie couldn't look at him. He didn't seem to want to know what happened. That was good, she thought. She honestly had no clue herself.

When he stopped the car, Jorie mumbled a 'thanks' as she began to open the door. He put a hand on her arm.

"Hey," he sighed, "don't go away like this. Are you alright?"

Jorie expected to feel the tears start, to want to sob and apologize and throw her arms around Bronx. But there was nothing.

She felt exhausted, her muscles weak, a dry mouth, but emotionally, she was empty.

"I'll be OK," she muttered, offering a forced smile. "Thanks again. I've got to get home." Jorie usually hated leaving things hanging, especially with him. It was just in her nature to want to resolve issues, iron out disagreements, and the ridiculous fight they had the night before still hung in the air. But before Bronx could say another word, she closed the door. They would eventually work it out, she knew. They always did.

True to form, Bronx was the first to apologize the next day when they talked. *Why does he always have to be so sweet?* Jorie wondered, aggravated. She was the one who got mad on the drive home from the gallery, took off without even talking things through with him, spent the night God-knows where, and then had the nerve to call him for a ride. She was the only one who even had anything to apologize for, and here he was telling her how sorry he was that things had gotten so out of control.

"Please, don't apologize , Bronx," she begged wearily. "It was me. I don't know what my deal is lately. I'm sorry." That was all she had the energy to say. All she seemed to do was screw up and have to keep telling everyone how sorry she was. And the sad truth was, she was never even really sure she meant it. All she knew was that she was tired, so tired and out of breath. It felt to Jorie like she had been holding her breath ever since her surgery. Hell, ever since she was 20 years old. When everything in her world turned upside down and suddenly nothing made any sense. She wondered if she was ever going to breathe again?

* * * * *

As another summer began, Jorie couldn't shake the feeling that something was coming. It was approaching the second anniversary of the first time she and Bronx had slept together, and the prospect of carrying on the lie she was living in felt like every pound she'd lost since her surgery had come back to rest on her shoulders. The only thing Jorie found solace in was sitting alone in the backyard in the afternoons, having a glass of wine and hoping the answers would come to her. As though God were hearing the prayers she didn't even know she was praying, the decision would be made for her soon enough.

It was the weekend of their annual barbeque, and Jorie tried to keep herself busy with the preparations. She felt anxious, and kept a bottle of her favorite white wine close by as she baked and put together salads for her guests. As the time of their arrival approached, she stopped even bothering to put the bottle back in the fridge between glasses. It was hardly worth the effort, since it was never on the counter long enough to get warm anyway.

Bronx sent her a text early Saturday morning, letting her know that he'd be running late, and that he loved her. She deleted it as soon as she read it, feeling guilty for erasing the sentiments that made her pulse race. Despite her dread at having to continue her deception, the fear of having Ryan discover the heartfelt message still scared Jorie. It was out of habit, and obligation, that she knew she wasn't ready to reveal the truth to her husband. Though she didn't know how she could continue on this way, the promise she had made to Ryan meant getting through this day just like any other.

Jorie smiled and let in guest after guest. Since this was the tenth anniversary of their barbeque, it seemed that not only had Ryan invited every person they'd included in the past, but that they all came. Jorie vaguely recalled discussing this with her husband a couple of weeks before, but her memory was fuzzy. She knew that she had probably been drinking at the time (because frankly, when wasn't she at this point?), and didn't feel like being reprimanded for her little "problem" causing another point of contention. Jorie simply smiled, commented on how popular their party had become, and put some more frozen appetizers in the oven.

It was getting close to dark out when Bronx arrived on his motorcycle. The sound of it pulling up in front of the house reminded Jorie of the night two years earlier when he'd come for his first barbeque. The butterflies let lose in her stomach as she recalled being alone with him in the bathroom, bandaging his hand. She was amazed that the memory of his hand on her neck could still make her light-headed, after so many incredible nights together. Gina, who was helping her clean up some of the food that had been outside during the meal, squinted her eyes and cocked her head.

"What are you grinning at?" she asked her friend, a slight smile on her face.

Jorie blushed, realizing she had been caught in the memory, and continued her work. "Nothing, just happy I guess," she said, still smiling.

"Yeah, I'd be happy too if I polished off that whole bottle of Dom," Gina said as she gestured to the empty wine bottle on the counter. Jorie shook it off, refusing to allow the comment to bother her. She knew her friend was worried, but believed that if Gina knew what she had been dealing with, she would understand. It pained Jorie to keep it from her, almost as much as it did keeping it from Ryan, but she was determined not to put her best friend in such a difficult position. Gina liked Ryan, and Jorie felt the less people who carried around her baggage, the better.

As if on cue, Bronx and Ryan walked into the kitchen from the front hall. Jorie smiled and said hi as they headed out onto the back patio where the rest of the guests were milling. Gina stopped dead where she stood, staring at Jorie.

"Girl, tell me I did not just see what I think I saw?"

Jorie immediately turned off any facial expression and shook her head. "What are you talking about?" Jorie asked. She didn't know why, but it was all she could do to keep from bursting out laughing.

"Jorie, are you messing around with that guy?" Gina whispered hoarsely, motioning towards the patio doors. She set down the stack of plates she was holding, afraid she might drop them.

Jorie smiled at her. "Well I'm not usually in the mood, but he is my husband so I sometimes I have to…"

Gina cut her off. "You **know** what I mean! Do you have something going on with Bronx? I saw that look you gave him. That was not, 'thanks so much for coming to our nice family barbeque.' That was, I don't know what it was but it was something." When Jorie looked down at her glass, Gina pressed harder. "Jorie, I have known you since junior high. What the hell is going on lately? Something is up with you!" Gina exclaimed, trying to keep her voice down while pointing outside.

Jorie had wanted to tell Gina on so many occasions, but didn't feel like it was lying since her friend had never directly asked her. Now she was torn. She didn't like keeping secrets period, but this had been eating at her for two years. Two years of not having anyone to talk to about how deeply in love she was, about anything Bronx had done for her, to her. After all the struggling to keep their affair a secret, having to keep every bit of it to herself, Jorie wanted this chance to let it out. Now that it was in front of her, she didn't know if she could do it.

Just as she began to open her mouth, not knowing what she was going to say, her neighbor Kayla came bursting in from the back yard. "Jorie, you need to come out here," Kayla said seriously.

Jorie and Gina looked at each other, momentarily forgetting their conversation, and bolted out the patio doors. The glow of the string lights and burning tiki torches lit up the yard, and for a second Jorie didn't know what Kayla had called her out for. Then she heard the elevated voices coming from the group of men gathered on the second level of the deck. Spotting Bronx and Ryan in the middle of the group, she rushed down the short flight of stairs and up to one of Ryan's co-workers.

"John, what the hell is going on?" she asked. With all the men crowded around the group, she couldn't see what was actually happening.

John whistled as he sucked in a breath, a smile on his face. "Oh boy. Chuck is drunk," he said. "Between you and me Jorie, he doesn't drink much, I think mostly because he doesn't handle it well. I don't know what he's pissed about, but he's got a bug up his ass about something."

Now Jorie heard Chuck swearing, almost yelling, and some of the other guys trying to talk him down. She pushed her way to the middle of the group. Jorie summoned all her patience and tried to speak calmly when she got to Ryan's side. "What's going on, Chuck?" she asked, attempting a smile.

Ryan put his hand up in Jorie's direction. "Stay out of it, Jorie. He's just had a little too much." Ryan turned his attention back to his inebriated boss. "Chuck, let's just go sit down for a while?" he suggested.

Chuck squinted and swayed on his feet. He shook his head, and shook his finger at Bronx. "No, I don't need to sit. This son-of-a-bitch needs to go. Do you hear me Ryan?" Chuck said, putting his hand on Ryan's shoulder and pulling him closer. "He's got no business being here," Chuck breathed, just an inch from Ryan's face.

"Look, man," Bronx said to Ryan, "I don't want to cause any problems. I'll just go." He glanced at Jorie, who willed every muscle in her body to remain still when they all screamed to throw her arms around him.

"Chuck, maybe I could make you some coffee…" Jorie began, switching her attention from Bronx's intoxicating gaze.

Ryan spun his head around, almost holding Chuck up with one arm. "Jor, please don't help," he insisted.

But as soon as he said it Chuck began laughing. "Oh yeah," he slurred. "She's a big help." At first he didn't seem to be making sense, but almost before he said another thing, Jorie knew what was coming. Chuck's face became as stone serious as she'd ever seen, and he pointed firmly at Bronx. "You know they're sleeping together, don't you?"

There was not another sound in the world for what seemed to Jorie like an eternity. All the guys at the party who had been quietly trying to get Chuck calmed down, every woman standing whispering in groups around the yard, even the crickets immediately stopped. Nobody moved, nobody spoke. It was as though nobody even breathed. Chuck broke the silence, leaning in closer to Ryan.

"Man, I'm sorry I didn't tell you before. We thought we shouldn't, you know." When he said that, several of the guys from Ryan's shop dropped their heads and looked at their feet. "But you deserve better man. It's not right. This bastard shows up at your home when he knows he's bangin' your wife," Chuck continued, his words slurring again. He caught himself on the railing when Ryan pushed the older man's hand off his shoulder. Ryan spun around and looked at his wife.

"Jorie?" was all he could get out. Though she closed her eyes to avoid the question, he could see the answer in the tear that ran down her cheek. Jorie shook her head slowly as she looked up at the sky, her hands laced behind her neck. It wasn't a denial of what Chuck just said; Ryan knew her well enough to know it was disbelief at the situation itself. He turned to Bronx. His face was as much of a give-away as hers had been.

"Get the fuck off my property," he said coldly to Bronx. Ryan began walking towards the house, stopping briefly next to his wife. "You can go with him."

Jorie and Bronx looked at each other, disregarding the fact that every set of eyes was on them. She knew she had to go after Ryan, but for a second Jorie needed to get lost in the blue eyes she couldn't get out of her mind since the first time she'd seen them. Never before had she wanted, needed to be in his arms, but the inappropriateness of an embrace at this moment was beyond obvious. She turned to follow her husband before she couldn't stop herself when she ran into Gina.

"Not now, Gina," Jorie pleaded as her friend began to open her mouth.

Jorie knew where Ryan would go, and found him right there in the study at the back of the house. He was the only one who ever went in there. He sat in his desk chair facing the window. "Ryan, I have to talk to you."

"Is what Chuck said true?" he asked, not turning around.

"Can I just explain some things?" she begged, walking closer to the desk.

Ryan spun in his chair, glaring at her with a rage she'd never seen in him before. "I asked you a question. Are you and Bronx…?" he trailed off with the question, unable to finish speaking the unspeakable.

Jorie kept her eyes locked on Ryan's; needing to get it out and at the same time feeling she owed him an honest answer. "Yes." His head dropped, and she saw tears forming in his eyes. "I'm so sorry," she whispered sincerely. She had never meant those words more in her life. "I don't…" Jorie couldn't finish what she was going to say. What could she say? There were a million things she could think of, and not one of them even came close to being enough.

Ryan turned back towards the window. "I mean it. I want you out of here, now, tonight." Jorie had never heard him so sad, so angry, and so defeated. She opened her mouth to argue with him, and realized she couldn't. There was nothing she could say in defense of herself, and the truth was she didn't want to. After two years of making excuses to get out of the house, there had never been a time when she wanted to escape as badly as she did at that moment.

Back in the kitchen she found Gina sitting on a bar stool, having her own glass of wine. Jorie poured herself one as well, glancing out the window the backyard. Only a small group of people remained, sitting around the deck table talking. She was sure it was about her, but didn't particularly care.

"Everyone left?" she asked Gina. "Shit, seems like the fun was just getting started." Jorie's attempt at humor was lost on her best friend.

"How could you not tell me this, Jorie?" Gina asked quietly.

Jorie's neck was getting sore from all the times her head had dropped in shame that evening. She shook her head and braced herself on the counter with both arms. "Gina, I'm sorry. It sucked to have to carry this around with me, and I honestly didn't want you to have it with you too. You can be pissed at me for not telling you, but did you really want to have to keep this from Ryan for two years?" Jorie saw the shocked look cross Gina's face when she revealed how long she'd kept the secret. Gina's surprise quickly turned to anger and disappointment.

"Well sure, that would have been 'unfair' of you to ask me to keep your dirty little secret," Gina said sarcastically. "Keeping it to yourself made a lot more sense than to stop screwing around on your husband! Jesus, Jorie, how the hell could you do this to your family?" She was up on her feet now, wine sloshing around her glass as her arms flew through the air. "Please tell me something, that Ryan beats you or that you were abused as a child? Something so that I get this, because this isn't you. The drinking, the affair, you haven't been yourself at all since you had that surgery."

Now it was Jorie's turn for sarcasm. "You're right, Gina, I should really try harder to figure out what's going on for *your* benefit, so you can be more comfortable with it. After all this really is about you!" Jorie grabbed her purse from under the counter, checking to make sure her keys were in it. "I've been trying to figure out what the hell is going on with me for two years, so as soon as I get it, you'll be the first person I call."

Gina called after Jorie as she made her way out the front door, but Jorie wouldn't stop. She was in her car and racing down the street as Gina came walking down the driveway. Jorie had two places to go, and she wasn't going to stop to explain herself to anyone else in the meantime.

Her first stop was at the liquor store where she picked up four bottles of wine. Then she headed downtown. There was only one place in the world she'd felt she wanted to be over the past couple of years. Now, when nobody else seemed to want her, she hoped she was still welcomed there.

Bronx opened the door before she even rang the bell. He held a bag of frozen vegetables to his eye. Jorie had never seen a more somber look on his face, and she almost burst into tears again when she realized he'd been hurt.

"What happened?" she croaked.

He shook his head, silent. Bronx pulled her towards him with his free hand, holding their bodies together as tightly as he could. She felt him shudder, and every horrifying event of the evening exploded in Jorie's brain. She sobbed onto his shirt until it was wet with tears as he kissed the top of her head over and over.

For the first time in their entire relationship, Jorie and Bronx lay together through the night without making love. They held each other as though their very survival depended on not letting go. Jorie let loose another torrent of tears when she saw the black puffy eye under the make-shift ice pack Bronx used. When her brain exhausted from going over the mess of the night, she slid into a fitful broken sleep.

She tried to call Ryan's cell several times the next morning, but there was no answer. Finally on the eighth call she heard hello, but it wasn't Ryan, it was Jack.

"Hi mom, where are you?" he asked.

"Mom's out for a little while. Is your dad there?" she asked hoarsely, exhausted and worn out from too little sleep and too much alcohol.

Jack said, "He just handed me the phone. Here dad, it's mom," she heard Jack say from a distance, obviously trying to hand the phone over to Ryan. Her son's voice came back on the line. "Mom, he can't talk right now. When are you coming home?"

Jorie wondered the same thing. "In a little while, buddy," she said, trying to sound more optimistic than she felt. "How are Brennan and Gracie?"

Jack began a long story about how his brother had taken over his video game and how Grace had knocked over all the castles Brennan had built out of Legos. Jorie was hardly listening. Her head pounded, and she was becoming more irritated by the minute. She cut her son off.

"Sorry baby, I need to get going. Tell daddy I'll call him later." With that she hung up the phone and began getting her things together.

"Where are you going?" Bronx asked.

Jorie didn't look up. "I have to go talk to him. I know he's pissed, but if he's not going to get on the phone I'll just have to go there."

Bronx sat on the couch and watched her scattered attempt at gathering up what things she'd spilt out of her purse earlier looking for a cigarette. "Do you really think that's a good idea?" He winced at the pain in his face as he spoke.

Jorie stopped and looked at him. She could hardly believe the problems she had caused, sure it was one of Ryan's co-workers who had taken the shot at Bronx. He hadn't complained once, and she knew it was because he believed he deserved it. He'd probably be out letting her husband take a few swings at him if his face didn't already hurt so badly.

"I know Ryan. He's going to be just as mad tomorrow and the next day, so it really isn't going to matter how long I put this off. Besides, I want to see my kids. He can hate me all he wants, but he can't keep me from seeing my kids."

Bronx was off the couch, holding Jorie in his arms before she knew what was happening. He didn't say anything else, but could sense he would have been happy for her to never leave his loft again. He also understood that she was a mom. She might not have been the best one up to this point, but she'd never felt so cut off from her own children before. Jorie had made the choice to spend her time with Bronx instead of her family many times over the past two years, but she'd never been told she wasn't "allowed" to see her kids. The truth was this terrified her more than Ryan never forgiving her, even more than never seeing Bronx again.

Twenty minutes later she pulled up in front of her house. It felt like a stranger's house, even though she'd only been gone a few hours. There was an eerie quiet for a Sunday morning. Usually the kids would be playing in the front yard, the lawn mower would be running, but there was nothing. Jorie shook as she got out of the car.

The kids were all playing quietly in the family room. After she gave them all hugs and the two younger ones resumed their game, Jorie asked Jack where his father was.

"He's in his study mom. He's not in a very good mood."

Jorie ruffled his hair and assured him dad was going to be alright. It just then occurred to her that the little boy she'd been raising was turning into a young man. It almost made her cry, because she wasn't ready for him to grow up, and because she realized she was missing it.

She had a quick drink from one of the half empty wine bottles still in the fridge from the night before. Even though it was only ten in the morning, Jorie was hoping it would stop her hands from shaking so badly.

Ryan was sitting in the chair, facing the large window in the back of the study, just as she had left him the night before. He didn't turn around when she walked in the door, and Jorie had a feeling of deja vue.

"Ryan?" she said quietly. He still didn't turn, but she could see he had on the same clothes as he'd worn to the barbeque. Jorie took a deep breath and tried again. "Ryan, I think we need to talk."

He finally turned and faced his wife. Jorie immediately saw that his eyes were red and puffy, and when he spoke she could smell the liquor on his breath. Ryan had probably been drunk fewer times than she could count on both hands the entire time they'd been married. Out of the corner of her eye she saw half a bottle of Jack

Daniels on the desk. She'd never seen him drink anything other than beer.

"You think we need to talk?" Ryan almost squinted to see her. "Do you really? Now you think we need to talk? I'm thinking maybe we should have talked oh, I don't know, quite a while ago." Jorie recognized the sarcasm she was so used to hearing come out of her mouth, but rarely her husband's. "If you're here to chat about your little romance, I think I got all the details I need from the guys."

Jorie had wanted to ask Bronx how Chuck could have known about the two of them, but she didn't feel she could take a fight with him right now too. Besides, considering the lengths he had gone to in an effort to help her hide the love affair from Ryan, it seemed unlikely he'd said a word to anyone at Ryan's shop. Something else was going on, and though she was sick with nerves, Jorie had to ask how he'd found out.

"How did Chuck know?" she asked somberly.

Jorie was half expecting another sarcastic response, but Ryan seemed more than willing to share everything he knew. "Well, it seems your boyfriend's boss had found out about the same time Bronx stopped working at our shop. He asked Chuck if he would prefer they pulled him from the job in the interest of keeping things 'civil.' I don't know if Chuck thought that would put an end to the whole thing or what, but we ended up with some dumbshit who wouldn't know a light socket from his asshole and apparently Bronx ended up with my wife."

Sitting gingerly on the edge of one of the office chairs, Jorie pressed on. The drink she had on the way in seemed to give her a little more confidence than she had walking in the house, and now she wanted things laid out on the table. She looked at her nails, the bracelet Bronx had given her after their first year together, and then looked at Ryan. He hadn't taken his eyes off her.

"I am sorry. I know that doesn't mean very much to you right now, but I don't know any other way to put it." She could say she'd made a mistake, that if she could take it back she would. Neither of these things was true. As much as she wanted to stop Ryan's pain, she couldn't talk about Bronx like he was some error she'd committed. Jorie had never been more in love with anyone, and minimizing that felt like a deliberate betrayal of everything they'd meant to each other. At the same time, she didn't want to rub any more salt in Ryan's wounds, so she shut her mouth and let him talk.

"Jorie," he began, his features softening, "I don't even know what to say." He rubbed his hands on his face. "I want so much to hate you right now. I really do. I just don't know how. All the years we've had together, three kids, I've never had one bad thought about you. I don't know how to go right to hate. But I don't know if I can really talk to you about this right now. I really don't know how to." He spun back around to face the window, and Jorie dropped her head realizing her husband of almost 13 years was crying.

She decided to give him the dignity of being left alone, and went back to the kitchen. After another quick drink, she decided to pack a bag for herself. As much as she hated the idea of being thrown out of her own house, Jorie didn't feel she could stay there the way things were. After stashing the bag in her car, she went back to Ryan's study. He hadn't moved.

"Why don't you take a nap and a shower? I'll stay with the kids until you're up, then I'll go." Jorie tried to sound matter-of-fact, desperately wanting to minimize the emotion of the situation at that point. As Jorie went back to the family room, she heard Ryan shuffling upstairs to sleep it off.

Four hours later, Jorie had played every game the kids had in their toy room, dressed up like a pirate and a princess, and finished most of the left over wine from the barbeque. She needed a nap herself, but forced her eyes to stay open on the drive back to Bronx's place. When she got there, she fell into his arms sobbing for the second time that day. It was partly the alcohol, but mostly the feeling that she was leaving her family behind for good without a choice in the matter.

Eleven

MONDAY DIDN'T FIND JORIE FEELING any better about the situation. Bronx came home early from work. At first he didn't want to tell her why, but eventually had to admit his boss had sent him home because of an "incident." It seemed he'd taken quite a bit of ribbing over the shiner he sported, and while he was willing to take that, he got into a fight with a co-worker who, as best as Jorie could decipher, had made a derogatory comment about her. Well, just when she didn't think she could feel any worse about herself. Bronx had always been the most even-keeled person she knew. Even Ryan said so. It took moving the world to get him riled up, and now thanks to her, he'd been involved in two fights in as many days. Jorie felt it was unlikely she would be asked to serve as a peace ambassador to the United Nations any time soon.

When the doorbell rang around dinner time, Jorie barely heard it from her spot on the deck. She'd spent almost all day out there, drinking wine and chain smoking. She had never smoked in Bronx's house, so it hardly seemed worth going inside. She was just going to want another one five minutes after putting out the last. She hadn't even smoked most of them. Light one, watch it burn out, and move on to the next.

Jorie was lost in watching the red end burn slowly towards the filter when Gina walked through the French doors that led out to the balcony. She barely glanced up at her friend, but did a double take when she realized Gina wasn't alone. Laney walked out the door behind her.

Her first instinct was to make a smart ass remark, but she didn't have the energy. Jorie returned her gaze to watching the cigarette burn out as the two women took seats across from her.

"Jorie," Gina started, "we came to take you out with us."

Jorie stifled a laugh. She shook her head and finally looked up at Gina. "I don't feel like going out."

"We're not going to a club," her best friend said softly. "Laney has a better idea."

She looked at the woman who had so inspired her just a few short years earlier. Now Jorie felt no inspiration, and none of the admiration she had felt when she first watched Laney's video on Dr. Cain's website. All she felt was defeated. "I'm not going to one of those support group meetings." If Jorie hadn't been able to discuss her struggles with food at the one and only meeting she'd gone to, she felt confident that there was no way she was going to be able to talk about the mess she was in now.

"We're not going there either. Now would you just get yourself dressed, please," Gina demanded. Jorie knew her well enough to know she wasn't leaving without getting what she wanted. It wasn't worth the fight to keep arguing with her. Jorie had no fight left in her.

An hour later the three women were walking into a church Jorie had never seen before. She was not a religious person, and became increasingly nervous that Gina and Laney were bringing her there for some sort of exorcism. Actually, she decided, it probably couldn't hurt. Whatever demons had taken over her brain were in full control now, and Jorie had no idea how to get them out on her own. She would soon find that was indeed their plan, though not in the way she was thinking.

They went into a room that was obviously used for child care, and Jorie became even more confused. Good God, she thought, were they the babysitters? It was immediately evident that they weren't there to do daycare. The room was full of adults, sitting around three circular tables and laughing. They looked up in unison when the women entered the room, almost as if it was rehearsed. Jorie was uncomfortable. She took a sip of the diet soda she'd brought in a gas station mug. It was the only thing Gina would let her bring along.

"Hey, Laney," greeted the man sitting at one end of the table. Others in the room smiled at her in recognition. As Jorie followed Laney and Gina around the table to three empty chairs, she saw a sign on the table. Overeaters Anonymous Meets Here it read. Now Jorie was really confused. As she sat next to her best friend, she leaned over and whispered to Gina, "What the hell, Gina? I don't have a problem overeating. I have no stomach, remember?"

Gina didn't look at her, but smiled at some of the other people in the room. "Just shut up and listen. It's an hour out of your life. What else did you have to do with your night anyway?"

Jorie tilted her head and raised her eyebrows. The answer was nothing.

"OK, let's get started," said the man who had greeted Laney. He opened the folder in front of him and began reading. While Jorie didn't much feel like being there, she thought concentrating on what these people were saying was preferable to listening to the voices in her own head. Wow, were they cranky!

As she listened to story after story about these people's struggle with food, Jorie's emotions got the better of her. Some of the things they were saying hit home for her, and she remembered going through the same things before her surgery. Even the ones that she couldn't personally relate to affected her. She had cried through most of the meeting, trying to blow her nose quietly in the back of the room and hoping nobody would look her direction. After she'd gone through all the Kleenex in her purse, Laney handed her a box off the table. Apparently this kind of thing was not uncommon, but that didn't make Jorie feel any better.

After the meeting, Jorie was approached by several people and given more hugs than she was comfortable with. She couldn't get out of the room fast enough and immediately lit a cigarette in the parking lot. Laney was busy talking with some of the other members as Gina and Jorie stood next to her car.

"So?" Gina asked as Jorie drew on her cigarette.

"So what?" Jorie countered, looking her friend in the eye. "I told you at the beginning I don't have a problem with food anymore. What do you want me to say?" Jorie felt like she'd fulfilled her obligation of going with them, and now all she wanted was to get back to Bronx and a bottle of wine.

Just then Laney walked up to them, spinning her key chain around on her finger. She didn't open the car though. She leaned on it and looked at Jorie. "I know what you're thinking. Your surgery took care of your food problem, so you don't need this. That's what I thought, too," she continued as Jorie nodded. "I was actually in OA before I had my bariatric surgery, and I didn't think I needed to keep coming after the weight came off. I figured I was 'cured.'"

"So why did you come back?" Jorie asked. She really didn't care about the answer, but figured the sooner they finished this conversation, the sooner she could get them to take her home. Actually, it was Bronx's home, not hers. But at the time it was all the home she had.

"This," Laney said, lifting the front of her shirt slightly. Jorie was a bit taken aback, but then leaned forward to inspect the scar which resembled her own plastic surgery scars. Only this was much more mangled and messy looking than her own smooth red line. She was disgusted and intrigued at the same time. Laney continued. "A couple of years after my gastric bypass I wanted my excess skin removed, but I had spent all the money I had on my first surgery, so I went to Mexico for this one," she pointed at her stomach. "They didn't make a mistake. I just had a regular complication from the surgery. But because I hadn't had it done in the US I couldn't go to my primary care doctor for follow-up, so it just went on until it got so bad I had to be hospitalized. When I got home I felt ugly and depressed, and then it hit me how much I had used food to cope with things like this." Laney pulled her shirt back down. "Jorie, I was almost in the same place as you are when somebody pointed out to me that I needed to get back to a meeting. Until then I thought I had licked it, but I found out that how much I ate wasn't the problem. It was how I related to food, and how I related to life without food. The overeating was just a symptom of my problem. Is this making any sense?" she asked when she saw the dazed look on Jorie's face.

Jorie was terrified to realize this really was making sense. She had gone into her surgery thinking it was going to solve so many problems in her life. She'd spent years wanting the weight off, but since she'd lost it, all she seemed to do was make decisions that hurt other people. For a minute she wanted to blame the surgery, but the reality was it wasn't about the surgery or whether or not she was thin or fat or anything in between. It was about how she had dealt with things in the interim, and Jorie was suddenly more ashamed than she been even the night of the barbeque. That seemed like light years away now, even though it had only been two days.

It was Gina's turn to address her best friend. "Jor, I called Laney not knowing any of this. It's not exactly something the hospital advertises on their bari site," she said, and Laney nodded. "I just thought maybe she could give me some advice, but I think she's done a lot more than that. I don't know how much you listened to in there, but I heard your story over and over. I've known you since we were 12. I've seen you go through so much in your life, but since you've lost your ability to use food to cope, you're using wine, Bronx…"

Jorie's head snapped up, her face flushed. "You've known about us for two days and all of a sudden you're an expert on our relationship?" She surprised herself with the venom in her voice.

Gina looked like somebody slapped her, but she kept on. "No, I'm not an expert Jorie, but I do know you. Like it or not, I do, and I'm telling you this as your friend. Whatever you have going on with him wouldn't have even started in your old life."

"You mean when I was fat?" Jorie hissed.

Gina shook her head, exasperated that she couldn't get through to her friend. "Look, I know you're pissed at Ryan and everyone else right now but…"

Laney interrupted the feuding friends. "Guys, I think we're getting a little off-topic here," she said calmly. Stepping in front of Jorie she faced her and put a hand on her arm. "You heard them say to try six meetings before you decide if this program is for you. I'm asking you to do that. I go to a few different ones, and I'm happy to take you to any. Do you want to try?"

Jorie looked down at her feet, the tears coming before she could stop them. She nodded, unable to speak. Besides Bronx, these were the only people who had offered to help her in the past 48 hours, and even she knew it was stupid to turn that down.

That week Jorie went with Laney to three more meetings, and even one on her own. She found that it was almost more comfortable to be there alone, not really knowing anybody and they not knowing her. She didn't talk at any of the meetings, but tried to listen to every word each person said. When she started to feel her mind wandering she tried to pull herself back into the room and focus on what the speaker was saying. Sometimes it was easier than others, but she walked out of each meeting feeling better than when she went in.

In the first few meetings Jorie didn't feel like she was making any real progress, but she knew she was comfortable in those rooms, amongst people who seemed to have dealt with the same problems as her. Some were better, and some were decidedly worse, but for the first time in as long as she could remember, there was no judgment being handed down on anyone. Having grown up dealing with her weight issue, Jorie constantly felt like all eyes were on her, like people were wondering what was wrong with her. Why couldn't she just eat like a normal person, be a normal weight? This feeling of being under a microscope had been what drove her to try so hard to become invisible. That lasted until the surgery, when she suddenly was the subject of good attention. It was very difficult for her to get used to, but she tried to enjoy it. Now it was becoming clear that she had handled it all wrong, and so many people seemed to be paying the price.

Jorie told her firm she wasn't going to take any jobs for a while, and they didn't ask any questions. Several of her co-workers had been at the now-infamous barbeque, and were well aware of her family problems. She needed the time to work things out at home, but at the same time was consciously grateful for not having to deal with the whispers and knowing looks at work. Despite the friendships she'd developed there, Jorie knew most of her colleagues just couldn't resist a good drama.

Ryan had been decent about letting her come over to visit the kids. Jorie's initial instinct was that she wouldn't leave her kids for anything, and either wanted to come back to the house or take them with her. Even though she knew he may not have been ready for it, she was sure Bronx would welcome her kids because of how much he loved her. In reality, neither of these plans seemed very feasible. Jorie wasn't ready to come home, and felt in her heart she never would be. She had hid the affair from Ryan for two years to spare him, and now that all seemed to be for nothing. There was no way to undo what she'd done to him, and as much as she hurt for the pain she'd caused, the feelings she needed to have for Ryan to work out their marriage just weren't there. Jorie often wondered if they had ever been.

After a few weeks of meetings, Jorie had heard over and over how important it was to get a sponsor to work her program. She had no idea how to go about doing this, and started shaking every time she considered asking someone as they suggested. There was one woman who had attended several of her meetings, and always seemed to have something to say that struck a chord with Jorie. This woman reminded her of a favorite aunt she'd had as a child, and one afternoon, at the end of a particularly emotional meeting, Jorie found herself talking to Rhea in the parking lot of the church where the meeting was held.

"How have you been holding up, honey?" Rhea asked.

Jorie took a drag of her cigarette and shook her head, tears still standing in the corners of her eyes. "I don't know. Every day is different. Sometimes every minute is different."

Rhea nodded her head in understanding. "Sometimes it's like that. I've seen you at quite a few meetings. That's the best place to start. Have you gotten some literature or done any reading? That always helps me get through the tough parts of the day."

This seemed to be the opening Jorie had needed, and she summoned all the strength she had left to walk through it. "I really haven't. I was actually thinking about getting a sponsor. Do you... do you think you might have some time for that?" she almost whispered the last part.

Rhea raised her eyebrows in contemplation, digging through her seemingly bottomless purse for a chap stick. "Possibly. I'm glad to see you're making it to a lot of meetings, but I need to know how much you really want to work a program. We can get together and talk a bit about how I usually work with my sponsees, and you can decide if it's something you want."

Jorie wasn't quite sure how to take this response. It wasn't a yes, but it wasn't a no either. She decided the best option was to meet with Rhea for coffee the next day and discuss exactly what this all meant. Jorie felt more comfortable with her than she had anyone else in quite a while, and didn't want to miss the opportunity to let this woman help her.

The next afternoon the two women met for coffee and made a bit of small talk. It didn't take long for Rhea to get down to business.

"Like I said yesterday, it's good that you're making so many meetings. I know you're pretty new to the program, so I want you to know how I usually work with my sponsees. Everyone has a different way they work the program, and I like to be upfront from the beginning so you know what you're getting into." Rhea had a slight smile on her face, but her tone told Jorie she was being completely serious.

Jorie just kept nodding, feeling like she was in an interview. She just wasn't sure who was interviewing who.

"I work from the How it Works in OA book, I will want to talk to you daily in the beginning, then maybe less as things move forward. You're going to have to be abstinent from food, just like an alcoholic has to quit drinking to really work your program seriously."

Jorie interrupted her. "That shouldn't be a problem. I had this bariatric surgery a few years ago, so I can't eat much."

Rhea shook her head, a knowing smile on her face. "That's the thing. Just because you had surgery doesn't necessarily mean you've been abstinent. Yeah, maybe you lost some weight, maybe a lot of weight. But we need to look at your food to see if there are still things going on that need to be changed. I don't work your program for you, but most people come into this brand new to a 12-step, and it can be confusing to figure out what kinds of things you really can't have. A drunk knows they can't drink alcohol, somebody in NA knows they can't use coke, but a food addict can't just give up food. Your food addiction isn't just about a weight problem. You probably noticed not everyone sitting in the meetings is overweight?"

Jorie had noticed that. She was actually pretty surprised to find that probably half of the people in every meeting she'd attended were either average or under-weight. Though she'd really never given any thought to OA before, in her mind she figured it would have been more like a Weight Watchers meeting. It definitely wasn't.

Rhea reached across the little wooden table and took Jorie's hand. Her smile put Jorie at ease before she even said anything. "Relax, sweetie," she said gently. "I know it's overwhelming, especially if there are other issues going on in your life that seem a lot bigger or more important than the food. But if you think you'd like to try this the way I've done it, I'm happy to work with you."

Jorie still wasn't sure what all of this meant. All she knew was that yet another person seemed to want to help and support her. Jorie was fairly convinced she didn't deserve it, but she was willing to accept it, which they told her was all she had to do for the time being.

The first task Rhea had given her was to document all the food she was eating each day. What exactly, how much, when she was eating it and so on. Jorie called her midway through the first day to ask if wine was considered a food.

Rhea paused after the question, and then slowly said, "Well, if you mean do you have to record it in your food journal, yes. If you mean can it be considered your food for the day, not so much. Jorie, are you drinking now?"

It hadn't occurred to Jorie that it was barely lunch time, being half way through a bottle of Dom might not seem right to your average food addict. But Jorie was feeling more and more comfortable with Rhea all the time, and she believed starting out lying to her sponsor was a little like paying a shrink and then telling them everything was fine every session. After so many years of lying and covering her tracks, Jorie was mentally exhausted. She just didn't have it in her anymore.

"Yeah," she said, barely above a whisper.

Jorie braced herself for a lecture, but Rhea just explained that it was important to document everything she put in her body, and to make sure she included the amounts. Jorie found herself relieved that she not only had told the truth, but that she wasn't being chastised for her actions. At least not by Rhea, even if she was still doing it to herself.

Bronx had been quietly supportive of Jorie's work with Rhea, which was little surprise to Jorie. Even the best meetings didn't compare to getting back to his place and curling up on the couch to watch a movie or talk about the day. Part of Jorie felt guilty that she was enjoying her time with Bronx so much. She wasn't at home with her kids to get them ready for bed and tuck them in. When these thoughts popped into her head, she tried to follow Rhea's suggestion and would write in her journal. Of course if she had a couple of drinks while she was writing, she felt better that much faster.

After just a couple of months of work with Rhea, Jorie grew closer to her than anybody in a long time. She had made it through the first three steps of the OA program, which were much the same at the steps of Alcoholics Anonymous, only regarding food rather than alcohol. Even though Jorie was far from having her problems resolved, she felt a bit better about herself. Late one Saturday morning she was contemplating this when Bronx came in from an emergency work project that had taken him out of the house at 7am.

"Wow, you're moving early," he remarked, finding Jorie showered, dressed and searching the apartment for her car keys. "Going to a meeting?"

"Yeah, but not my regular one. Rhea is speaking at a meeting at noon and she asked me to come to it and it's half way across town," she rambled distractedly.

"Are these what you're looking for?" he asked, pulling her keys off the side of her purse. When she reached for them, he noticed her hands were shaking. "You haven't had anything to drink today," he stated somberly.

Despite, or maybe because of, the almost concerned sound in his voice, Jorie snapped back at him. "No actually, I haven't. There's nothing left to drink, and this is an AA meeting, not OA. So there, I've blown Rhea's anonymity to tell you that no, I haven't drunk anything today. I didn't want to show up at an AA meeting with booze on my breath!" Jorie snatched the keys from Bronx, who stood silently staring after her as she tromped out of the loft.

By the time she arrived at the meeting, Jorie felt even worse. She had a headache, her skin itched and she felt terrible about barking at Bronx, who, as usual, was just trying to help. She was relieved to see Rhea, but inwardly willed the hour to pass as quickly as possible so she could get out of that room. Jorie had never been to an AA meeting, but quickly realized it was formatted much like her regular OA meetings. She tried to focus on the words the chairperson was saying, forcing herself to look for differences between the two meetings as a way to keep her mind on something besides the snail-speed hands on the clock or her leg, which bounced uncontrollably.

Once it was Rhea's turn to get up and tell her story, Jorie had an easier time paying attention. She had heard much of it at the OA meetings and through their sponsorship work together, but had never heard the whole thing from beginning to end. Rhea's alcoholism was never much the topic of conversation, and Jorie was fascinated by how profoundly it had affected Rhea's life. Her sponsor spoke of things she had done while drinking, things she hadn't done, and discussed how her addictive cycles didn't end when she stopped using alcohol. She then turned to food, and shared about her struggles with that addiction as well. Jorie was surprised to hear her discuss her food addiction so thoroughly at an AA meeting. She was even more shocked that many of the people at the meeting were nodding their heads in understanding as Rhea spoke.

As the chairperson began the closing of the meeting, Rhea leaned back from where she sat in the row in front of Jorie and whispered, "Stick around, we're going to lunch." Jorie nodded, inwardly disappointed that she couldn't just swing by the liquor store and then go home to apologize to Bronx. The months she'd spent working with Rhea meant so much to Jorie. She could pull it off for a little while longer.

Jorie hung out by the door to the meeting room, smoking and waiting for Rhea to get through hugging seemingly every person in attendance. Her hands still shook when Rhea finally emerged from the building with another woman and the meeting's chairman. As though reading her mind, her sponsor suggested they go to a local chain restaurant with a patio for lunch. Jorie knew they served alcohol, and she couldn't have been more relieved.

Twelve

AS SOON AS THE SERVER asked what he could get them to drink, Rhea looked pointedly at Jorie and told her to have a glass of wine. She didn't need to be told twice, and three drinks later Jorie started to feel her body begin to calm down for the first time that day. The fact that she was drinking at a table full of recovering alcoholics didn't seem to bother any of them in the least, and Jorie was grateful for that. She had originally thought she would make it through lunch alright, but now realized that she needed a drink more than she knew. After a couple of tentative bites at her salad, Jorie was no longer hungry and ordered another drink.

Rhea was the next one done with her meal and sat back in her chair. She looked at Jorie and asked what she thought of the meeting.

"It was cool," Jorie said. "Different than I thought it would be, but cool."

"It is different. You probably won't find another meeting like it in town." Rhea took a deep breath and sat forward. "Jorie, have you ever heard the term addiction transfer?"

Jorie shook her head. She had learned a lot of lingo in her time at OA, but this was a new one for her.

The other woman from the meeting, Char, lit a cigarette and began to explain. "It's usually something people think of happening after weight loss surgery, though it can really happen any time. It just basically means you've overcome one addiction but taken on another."

"This meeting we just came from is mostly attended by people who have experienced an addiction transfer," said Dale, the lone man at the table. "Of course, the WSO prohibits us from placing that title on the meeting, or restricting anyone from attending who has the desire to stop drinking. However, it is well known as a place for addicts who have found themselves afflicted with this particular ailment to meet once a week with like-minded people."

Jorie shook off the urge to ask Dale if he'd eaten a dictionary for breakfast, and asked, "Why would the World Service Organization care what you call your meeting?"

Rhea took over at that point. "Because Tradition 3 says the only requirement for membership *is* a desire to quit drinking. We can't restrict our meetings, nor do we want to. But that's not really the point of why we're talking to you about this. You know that I'm an alcoholic, and I wanted you to hear the story about how I started eating after I gave up drinking because I needed to fill that gap, and I wasn't working my program the way I should have been. Dale here," she continued, motioning to the man on her left, "smoked pot, then went on to alcohol and coke. And Char had a bariatric surgery like you, and then started drinking." Rhea slowed her speech and leaned forward, looking pointedly at Jorie. "Now most people who have weight loss surgery don't experience addiction transfer, but most people who suffer from addiction transfer have had some type of weight loss surgery. Does that make sense?"

Jorie gave Rhea her best sarcastic smile. "Is that like one of those Zen riddles?"

Just then Jorie looked up to see Bronx walking up to their table. Her heart usually soared when he walked into a room, but this time it sank like a boulder. After a quick round of introductions and hellos, Bronx pulled a chair up next to Jorie as she turned her attention back to Rhea.

"So what, is this some sort of intervention?"

The older woman laughed lightly and shook her head. "No, an intervention would be a lot more uncomfortable. This is lunch."

"But you think I have a drinking problem? That's what you all think?" she demanded, looking around at everyone at the table.

"Do you think your drinking is a problem?" Rhea asked.

"Not for me," Jorie said seriously. She looked over at Bronx, who's eyes were glued to her face. "And you're in on this too?"

"J, this isn't some conspiracy against you. Rhea asked me to come and I wanted to be here. You know I love you."

Jorie shook her head and sat back hard in her seat. She felt like a caged animal on display, with all eyes on her, waiting for her to act. She looked again at Rhea. "This is total bullshit Rhea. I don't need this."

Dale spoke in his calm tone. "Jorie, can you describe what exactly it is that keeps you from wanting to take advantage of this opportunity? Is it the rehabilitation center, foregoing the alcohol itself…"

Jorie didn't let him finish his question. The reality of what he said was an icy slap across her cheek. Her eyes the size of soccer balls, she looked from Rhea to Bronx and back. "Rehab? Seriously, you guys expect me to go away to the spin-and-dry and for how long? Why don't I just sign the kids over to Ryan now?"

At that comment Rhea looked at Bronx and nodded her head. "Tell her."

Bronx took Jorie's hand and looked down. "You know Paul, the guy we have working over at Ryan's shop now?" Bronx met her eyes. "He's, uh. Well, he's heard some things there."

"What kind of things?" Jorie asked, her eyes narrowing.

Bronx sighed. "Ryan wants the kids. And J, the way you're drinking, he's going to get them."

Jorie pulled her hand away and stood up so quickly she almost knocked the table over. She grabbed her sunglasses and quickly put them on, noticing that people seated near them were now looking their way. Trying to keep her voice low she said, "Well fuck him.

And you know what, fuck you guys too." She spun on her heel, nearly sending her chair flying, and headed straight for the exit.

Jorie was lighting a cigarette outside the main doors when Bronx caught up with her. Though she was forever finding herself torn between wanting to be mad at him and wanting to grab him and hold on for dear life, this was not one of those times. Jorie thought this might be one of the few times she really felt let down by Bronx. Why would he be involved in this little ambush by Rhea, another person she thought she could trust? Jorie tried to walk towards her car, but he wouldn't have it.

"J, I know you're pissed, and that's fine. But you also know I wouldn't have done this if I didn't think it was pretty much necessary. I don't want to see you lose your family any more than you already have. And more than that, I don't want to see you lose yourself."

Jorie put her hand up to stop him. "Why don't you just say it? You think I'm an alcoholic."

"I think you're an alcoholic," Bronx said matter-of-factly.

"No I'm not!" Jorie insisted. "Christ, I've had a bit of stress going on in my life lately, in case anyone missed that. Yeah, I probably have a drink too many from time to time, but I'm trying to get through all this shit the best I can."

Bronx looked hurt. "It's not all shit, Jorie. And if you think about it, it's not just since all this started with Ryan and you being out of the house. You've been drinking this way most of the time we've been together."

Jorie's sarcastic smile was back. "You think that's a coincidence? So is this your "amends" for sleeping with me when I was married to your friend and turning me into a raging alcoholic who can't deal with the simplest problem without a drink? You're going to fix me? Get me into treatment so you don't have to feel guilty about any of this? Well don't bother. I officially absolve you of any responsibility, for me or anything else." Jorie threw her hands up in the air for emphasis, causing customers who were going in to glance at her out the corners of their eyes and move a little quicker.

Rhea came up to the couple, her hands crossed under her chin. "Jorie, I know this is going to sound strange based on your reaction in there. But nobody has really asked you straight out; are you willing to go to treatment?"

Jorie walked to the end of the sidewalk away from the door to the restaurant. There she stopped and sat down hard. She had intended to go to her car and get as far away from this conversation as possible. Something stopped her, right there at the end of that strip of concrete. She pulled her knees up to her forehead and cried like there was nothing good left in the world. Jorie knew she'd had plenty of low points over the past two years, but had never felt as far at the bottom of the abyss as she did sitting on that sidewalk, sobbing. The two people who she trusted most in the world, who had both been more real with her than she'd ever been able to be with herself, were both at her side. They had again offered her help, and she didn't have the energy to fight it anymore.

When she calmed enough to speak, Jorie put her chin on her knees and looked straight ahead. "OK, I've seen the shows. So what, you stick me on a plane to some place in the middle of the desert?"

Rhea chuckled softly. "Well not exactly. Bronx actually has something set up here in the state. I think just an hour or so from here?"

Jorie looked at Bronx, who's ice-blue eyes rendered her almost immobile. "It's a great place. The staff is very good, cool. You'll like them." He read her puzzled stare and answered her question before she could ask it. "It's the place we put my dad."

Her jaw dropped a bit, and Jorie shook her head. "You never told me your dad was an alcoholic."

"Really?" Bronx said. "Fascinating story. You'll love to hear it, someday." He stood up and held out his hand to help Jorie. She got to her feet, as did Rhea. "Right now we should get your stuff and go."

"Now? Right now? I want to see my kids before I go."

Bronx led her to his pickup. "No problem. I called Ryan, and he's expecting you to come by."

Jorie was stunned by how the events that were unfolding, but none more so than to hear that Bronx had called her husband to arrange for her to say goodbye to her kids. She imagined that was an incredibly hard call to make, and tears welled in her eyes as she climbed into the truck. The golf ball in her throat kept her from speaking, but she knew by the look on his face that she didn't need to say anything.

A thought suddenly occurred to her. "Shit, my car is here!"

"We'll come back for it later," Bronx said. "We're just going to stop by the loft and get your bag. Then we'll go by the house so you can see the kids, and Rhea and I will get the car after we get you settled in."

Jorie raised her eyebrows, impressed at his control of the situation. She felt nervous as she began her last question. "Bronx, can we get… I mean, can we stop…" Jorie couldn't get the words out.

He looked at her, putting the truck into gear and motioned to the extended cab. "Look."

She turned around and found a paper sack on the floor behind his seat containing three bottles of her favorite wine. Jorie relaxed immediately. If it was going to be her last day to drink, she thought she'd go out swinging. But how did he know that's what she was going to ask?

Once again he read her mind. "I've done this before," he said somberly.

Jorie made it through much of the first bottle by the time they had packed up a small bag and started for her house. Her house. The idea almost seemed foreign to her now. Neither she nor Ryan had done anything formally. No separation papers were filed. They hadn't even discussed getting divorced. Jorie wasn't really sure why.

She knew there was little chance they were ever going to recover their marriage. He seemed so angry with her all the time, and though she knew they were technically not living together because of her affair, in her heart she felt they hadn't been together for years.

As they parked in front of the house, Jorie began ringing her hands. She had never been so nervous about walking to that front door. Not even the day after the barbeque when she came over to talk to Ryan. That day she felt numb, but now it seems as if her body was trying to turn itself inside out. She didn't know how to say goodbye to her kids for a month. Jorie worried they were going to be scared and confused. She certainly was.

"Are you coming with me?" she asked Bronx as he put the vehicle in park but made no motion to get out.

"I don't think that's a good plan," he responded.

Jorie knew he was right, but she felt so much more at ease when he was in the same room with her. This was definitely something she was going to have to handle on her own. She shook as she pulled the handle on the pickup door, not from needing a drink but from needing courage. "How much time do I have?" she asked.

"How ever much you need," said Bronx.

An hour later, Jorie came out of the house her family had shared for the past ten years. Her eyes were red and swollen, and her shaking seemed to have taken over her entire body. She climbed into Bronx's 4x4 without a word. He grabbed her hand, and she squeezed back with the little strength she had left.

Thirteen

TWO AGONIZING HOURS LATER JORIE had finished off her bottles of wine, they'd picked up Rhea and were walking in the front doors of the treatment center. Most of the check in process was a complete blur to Jorie. She was fairly drunk at this point, and the sheer terror of the situation seemed to be manifesting itself as a catatonic state. Jorie stared at the papers on the desk next to her as Bronx and Rhea passed over her bag, a list of her 'safe' foods for the dietitian (leave it to Rhea to think of that), and the three of them listened to the basic rules of the center. Jorie didn't much care that she wasn't allowed any phone calls for the first few days, that she would be given meds to deal with the withdrawal symptoms or that she had group sessions starting the day after next. All she wanted to do at this point was either have another drink or go to sleep. It seemed the former wasn't going to happen in this place, so all that was left was the sleep.

Jorie's time in treatment seemed to move slowly at first. Though she had originally been resistant to the idea, once she was there it began to feel right. When Jorie had been so desperate to have her weight loss surgery, she thought she could never possibly want to be that same person. She had hoped to leave that woman behind, to start over new, thinner, happier. Now it was becoming clear to her that she had just let her mind go from one foggy reality marred by overeating to another distorted by alcohol. Jorie didn't know what part of her life had ever just been real, but the idea of discovering it intrigued her.

Group sessions were the hardest for Jorie. She found the embarrassment of all that she had done since she'd started drinking was much more raw without the buffer of the booze. Sitting in a little room discussing her darkest secrets with a counselor was not the highlight of her day, but at least that was just one other person. Group was a much scarier proposition for Jorie. But soon after arriving, she found that there was one event that made her even more nervous…Family Day.

All she heard from other people in the program was how much they couldn't wait for their kids, spouse, siblings, friends, significant others to come and take their minds off the fact that they were in rehab. Jorie, on the other hand, was completely terrified. And torn. She was deeply depressed at the idea that she couldn't see Bronx, but Jorie couldn't imagine giving up the chance to see her kids. It was the longest she'd ever been away from them. Just a couple of years earlier there would have been no doubt about who should come to visit her. Just a couple of years earlier she wouldn't have been in that place, or in that position.

"Hey, baby," Bronx breathed into the phone when Jorie called him that week. She leaned her head against the wall by the phone and closed her eyes. She hadn't realized how hard this was going to be until she heard his voice.

"Hey, yourself," she managed to get out. Jorie held the mouthpiece under her chin with one hand and put the other hand on her the back of her neck. "How are things?"

"Things are good. It's lonely without you here though. How are you doin?"

Jorie made small talk until her time on the phone was almost up. She had considered not even bringing up family day, but then remembered his dad had been in this very facility. He had to already know.

"Hey, you know we have this Family Day thing coming up, which, well you probably already knew that." Jorie was stumbling through every word. "I, um, I really want to see you. I miss you a lot, ya know. I just. I think it would be weird. I mean, Ryan has to be here because he has to bring the kids." There was a silence on the line. "Are you mad?" Jorie almost whispered.

Bronx seemed to be thinking, took a deep breath and said slowly, "No, I'm not mad. I mean, I want to be there. But I get it. Don't worry about it." His tone seemed cold to Jorie, though she wasn't sure if it really was or if it was in her head.

"I'm sorry, babe," she said. As usual he took her disappointment in stride, and as usual, it irritated her a bit. "Look, I've got to get off. Call you tomorrow?"

Bronx agreed, and they ended their conversation. Jorie was relieved the hard part was over. Now she just had to call Ryan and let him know what day to come with the kids

Ten minutes later Jorie hung up the phone slowly, her eyes the color of the red and white Diet Coke can she held in her trembling hand. Her friend Erin was just walking though the commons where the phones were located and noticed Jorie.

"Sweetie, what is it?" she asked, putting an arm around Jorie's shoulders.

"My, um," Jorie cleared her throat. "My husband isn't bringing my kids for Family Day. He doesn't think this is a good place to see me."

"Shut up!" Erin said in disbelief. "Really? I think drunk and in jail would be a bad place for them to see you. But here? Not so bad. What's his deal?"

Jorie shook her head. She knew exactly what his deal was. He was still as angry as he'd been the night he found out about her affair with Bronx, and it occurred to Jorie in that moment that he might never get over it. She was reluctant to believe what Bronx said at the restaurant, that Ryan would try to take her kids away from her if she didn't quit drinking. The idea scared her, but the fact that Ryan could ever do anything that hurtful to her seemed unfathomable. Jorie had never before let herself believe he was capable of causing her that kind of pain. She could now see that she had underestimated him, and depths to which he'd go to punish her for what she'd done.

Not feeling like participating in group, Jorie went out the back door of the facility to the garden area where there were several lawn chairs in various stages of wear. She found one where she could put her feet up. Jorie lit a cigarette, and tears formed in her eyes again as she recalled the conversation with Ryan on the phone minutes before.

"Hello?" he answered cautiously, as though he didn't immediately recognize the number but could guess who was calling.

"Hey," Jorie started, realizing she didn't know exactly how to ask him about coming to family day. When she started dialing, she just naturally expected he would bring the kids and come. Once she heard his voice though, she was snapped back to the reality of the situation that she wasn't really like his wife any longer. She couldn't just call him up and inform him of their weekend plans. Jorie was going to have to ask him to do her a favor, and the idea made her feel at once resentful and terrified.

Ryan let out a sigh and said "hey" back, almost sounding disappointed. It occurred to Jorie at this point that it might be an even more difficult feat than she had imagined. Well, if it was going to suck, she decided to treat it like taking off a bandage. She would just get it over with.

Her head hung as low as it could go, Jorie took a deep breath. "Um, this weekend we have this Family Day thing. It's for everyone, you know, and I'd love to see the kids. I mean, I would hope that you guys could all come?" She didn't want to give him too much encouragement that she might really be missing him. In fact one of the main advantages to being at the center for her had been that she hadn't had to deal with Ryan in days.

There was a long pause, and just as Jorie was about to ask if he was still there, Ryan spoke. "I don't think so, Jor. I don't want the kids to see you there, and who knows what other kind of people are around. I'm just not sure it's good for them right now."

Jorie had considered that this might be his initial reaction. "Well look, it's not so bad here. I mean the people are cool, and it's pretty comfortable. Like a hotel really," she said gently.

Ryan didn't respond for some time, and Jorie was again afraid he had hung up. Finally he breathed heavily into the phone and said coldly, "I really don't feel like seeing you. Or him…" He trailed off like he wanted to say more, but couldn't or shouldn't.

"I asked Bronx not to come," Jorie said softly. It was painful to hear herself say those words.

The pause wasn't as long this time, and Ryan sounded even sharper when he did speak. "You didn't need to bother. We can't be there."

"Ryan…" Jorie began.

"You can call and talk to the kids tomorrow afternoon, Jorie. They're all down now. I have to go." And with that he hung up the phone.

Jorie blew out cigarette smoke, watching it intensely and shaking her head. She knew Ryan was mad, furious still even after all these months apart. In fact, some days it seemed their relationship was becoming more acrimonious. Originally Jorie thought that time would heal some of the pain she had caused, but for Ryan, knowing she and Bronx were still together seemed to make things worse. Maybe he had hoped things with them would just fizzle out. Jorie wanted a drink more than any time since she'd come to the rehab center. She pulled her feet up on the chair and buried her face in her knees, praying for serenity.

Too embarrassed to call Bronx back after she'd asked him not to come to Family Day, Jorie moved through the next day in an emotional black hole. She didn't feel anything. She refused to talk during group, didn't eat and took every opportunity to sit outside and smoke. As had become her habit, she lit cigarette after cigarette, seldom smoking more than half but watching them burn as though they were the most interesting thing ever.

"Jorie!" her counselor called. It took her three more tries before Jorie took notice. "Can you come into my office, please?" Debbie's question sounded more like an order, and Jorie knew she didn't have the option to answer no. She had nothing better to do, so she put out her cigarette and shuffled into the counselor's office.

Debbie sat in the chair across from the couch where Jorie sat, her feet pulled up underneath her. "So, two days without participating in group. What's that about?"

Jorie picked at a small snag next to her in the couch cushion. "I don't know. Just didn't have anything to say I guess."

"Hmm," Debbie began, "did you set a new record for resolving all your issues? Maybe we'll have to put a picture of you in the lobby."

Jorie shook her head. She liked Debbie, and knew she was just kidding. That day Jorie didn't feel like joking around. "My family… is not coming…to Family Day." She took in a deep breath and let it out hard.

"And what is that about?"

Jorie stopped pulling the lose thread and looked at Debbie. "I guess my husband is still pretty pissed. Whatever. Fuck it." Jorie rubbed her hands over face and lean forward on her knees. "So that's the problem. So now what?"

"Why are you asking me?" Debbie laughed. "This doesn't sound like something either of us has control over. You're here to work your program. The question is, now what are you going to do? Are you going to waste the time you have left moping around or blowing off group because you're pouting? It sucks, but that doesn't mean you don't do the work."

Jorie was vaguely aware that she had developed a mostly "bad attitude" at the rehab center. That's what she would have called it if one of her children had been so defiant and uncooperative.

She glanced out the window of the bright sunny office, internally debating whether or not she was ready to let go of it.

The next few days passed quickly for Jorie. She was dreading the weekend, but tried to keep herself busy enough that she seldom thought about it. Sunday morning after breakfast she was lacing up her tennis shoes to go out for a long walk around the grounds when there was a knock on her door.

Rhea poked her head in the room. "Hey lady, up for some company?"

"Hey!" Jorie almost shouted. "What are you doing here?" she asked in shock as she embraced her friend.

"Well I wouldn't normally butt in on Family Day, but I stopped by your house to give these to Ryan to bring up to you," Rhea said, holding up a bag of peaches from her yard. Her voice dropped. "He said he wasn't coming." She tilted her head and put hand on Jorie's arm. "I'm sorry sweetie. I tried explaining how important it was. He's just...so... I don't know."

Jorie nodded silently, and gave Rhea another big hug. "Thank you," was all she could manage to choke out. *This is what it would be like if my mom or Addie were here*, she thought both wistfully and sadly.

The two women sat near the small pond downhill from the main building. For the next hour they discussed everything that had been going on with both of them, in their personal lives and in their recovery. Rhea told Jorie how she'd run into Laney at a day retreat. Laney knew of Jorie's rehab stay from Gina, and asked Rhea to pass along her best. Jorie wouldn't have met Rhea if it wasn't for Laney getting her involved in OA, and if it weren't for that program she would still be sitting at Bronx's apartment, crying in her wine. Or worse.

Just as Jorie was about to suggest they get some lunch before the afternoon group session, she noticed Rhea smiling and looking past her shoulder. Jorie turned to see Bronx walking down the hill towards the women. The sight of him never failed to accelerate her pulse, but that day it seemed to stop her heart. She wanted to run up the hill and throw her arms around him, but she was frozen in place. There was no way to stop the tears from coming, and when he reached the bench where they were sitting, Jorie couldn't bring herself to speak. She rose slowly, and buried her face in his chest as she had done so many times, the quiet desperation of the moment overwhelming her spirit. He was there, as he always was.

The three of them passed through the unseasonably warm afternoon of fall, laughing and talking about the mundane. It was a relief for Jorie, who had felt her days of counseling and group sessions were endless hours of reliving pain and fighting demons. She didn't ask why he had come. She knew him well enough to know it wasn't without invitation, and she knew Rhea well enough to know that a quick phone call after discovering that Ryan wouldn't be there was all it would take. Jorie recognized the irony that this man, who had taken so much time away from her children and been willing to aide her in committing adultery in the highest form, would have never disrespected her family by visiting her while they were there when she'd asked him not to.

After supper, as dusk began to settle over the peaceful hills that surrounded the recovery center, Rhea gave Jorie a powerful hug and said her goodbyes. She hated driving at night, and it was a more than an hour to her home. Jorie hugged back equally hard, without the words to tell the elder woman how much the day had meant to her. Rhea seemed to sense it though, and squeezed Jorie's hands after the embrace.

"I'm proud of you, kiddo," she said with a tight smile. She held back her own tears, and turned to get into her car before they came on in full force. Rhea rolled down the window part way and blew Jorie a kiss as she pulled away. Jorie was touched by the gesture, not just because it came from somebody to whom she owed her life. If her kids had been there, it would have been how they would have said goodbye, too.

Bronx locked his hand with hers, and suggested they take another walk down by the pond before he had to go as well. Jorie thought she should insist that he get home and get some sleep. It had been an emotionally draining day for all of them. But she couldn't bear the thought of being left all alone, and eagerly agreed to the walk. As the two of them moved quietly around the inky water, darkened by the disappearance of the sun, Jorie was struck by a profound sadness. At first she thought it was the fact that he would be leaving her soon, but somehow that didn't seem to be it. She couldn't put her finger on it, but it was there. A looming feeling that some cosmic change was occurring, and it couldn't be stopped. She pushed it aside…shoved it, actually. There would be time to consider its connotation later. For now, Jorie was determined to be present in each moment with Bronx while he was still there with her.

"I know you didn't ask," Bronx began, "but you know that I wouldn't have come. I mean, if he would have…" He trailed off, seeming concerned that what he was saying might be hurtful. Jorie smiled. She understood.

He kissed her gently next to the unmoving water, one hand behind her head as though she might just pass away from him in a wisp of smoke. Jorie felt it again, the jolt of finality that flashed around them. She discounted it for a second time, brushing it off like a stray hair tickling her neck. Many times when he held her and kissed her, she had wanted desperately for time to stop forever. Now she prayed to the God she was coming to understand, to let her hold on just a little longer. She wasn't ready to let him go, but despite her most valiant efforts, the clock continued to move ahead.

Fourteen

TWO DAYS AFTER JORIE CELEBRATED Family Day with her new "family," a large envelope arrived for her at the center. She tore into it, recognizing her home address in Ryan's handwriting from across the room. It was full of bright, colorful pictures that Grace had made for her, drawings Brennan had done of his favorite cartoon characters, and a homemade card that Gracie had obviously had some help in creating. She broke into an even wider grin, noticing that even Jack had managed to scrawl his name across the bottom of the card that said, "We miss you tons Mom. Come home soon!" Ryan had thrown in a hastily written piece of scratch paper, saying he thought some of the kids' art work might brighten up her room, and that they had been working hard on putting together this packet for her. She would have rather that he'd brought it to her, but decided she wasn't going to dwell on that right then. This was going to be a good day.

Jorie continued to plod along through the 12 step program that was laid out by the center, constantly amazed at the people she had become so close to in such a short period of time. It occurred to her that she might know more about some of them than she did about Bronx or even Ryan. And they weren't good things. They were things that would make you think, "Yeah, this is a person I wouldn't want to be friends with for any length of time." But they *were* her friends, and she tried hard to remember the tradition that told her to place principles before personalities. That wasn't always easy.

"You're shaking your head, Phil. Do you have something you want to discuss with the group?" Tara asked one afternoon near the end of Jorie's third week. Jorie liked Tara on a personal level, but she thought all the woman's counseling degrees and experience should have made her think better of asking Phil if he had something to share. Phil always had something to share.

"It's just bullshit," Phil began. *Here we go*, Jorie thought. "I mean, it's the same bullshit we hear every session. She doesn't want to get real about anything she's done. It's the same whining about her kids every day, but she doesn't want to really get to the heart of the problem…her part in it."

Phil was referring to was Mandy. This was Mandy's fourth time in rehab, and she had a stack of AA and NA chips to prove it. The problem was none of them represented more than six months clean and sober. Her four kids were split between her family members and their biological fathers (three of them) and if Mandy washed out of this treatment cycle, she would be going to jail for a couple of years at least. Phil was right about one thing; Mandy discussed little of the details of her problems in group. Jorie only knew as much as she did because they were roommates.

Over the murmurs and rustling of some of the other group members, Tara tried to regain control of the session by reminding Phil that there wasn't supposed to be crosstalk and feedback. They were there to discuss their individual struggles without worrying about being judged.

Phil shook his head. "That's fine for a meeting, but this is group. Aren't we supposed to be helping each other? I just think she needs to be called on her own shit."

This started an even louder exchange, with several voices now chiming in about Phil's comments, some asking who he was to be judging anyone, and some seeming to contend he was allowed to have his own opinion. Jorie, who had been concentrating as hard as she could on a hangnail she'd started picking earlier that day, closed her eyes and tried to block out the noise. It was a technique she'd employed though most of her group sessions, and it had worked pretty well, until that day. That day, she finally felt she had something to say.

"It's not bullshit!" And though she had the emphasis of real emotion in her tone, Jorie's voice was barely above a whisper. Even still, the room fell almost instantly silent.

Tara was the first to recover from the surprise of Jorie's first spoken words in group. Afraid she'd scare Jorie back into her silent hole, Tara asked her as flatly as she could, "Why do you say that, Jorie?"

For a second, Jorie wished she could take back her words. It occurred to her, now that they were out there, people were going to expect more to follow. Talking had never been something she'd struggled with in her life, but since confronting her demons at her very first Overeater's Anonymous meeting, she found it harder and harder to speak in front of these kinds of groups. Coming to the center had almost driven her into a monk-like silence that she either couldn't or didn't want to escape from. It felt both terrifying and freeing at the same time. But now it was over, and she knew she had something to contribute.

"It's not bullshit," Jorie repeated, this time a little louder. "I'm scared about who I'm going to have to face when I go back too. Who isn't? Who wouldn't be scared of having to fix the kinds of mistakes we've made? I've made," she corrected. "I don't know what is more scary…facing the people I KNOW I screwed or the ones I can't even remember. Jorie was acutely aware that all eyes in the room were on her, but she kept going. "You think it's bullshit for Mandy to worry about what her kids are going to think of her?" she asked, looking directly at Phil. "I think its bullshit that I have to worry about what my kids already think of me. I think it's bullshit that I have to remember getting so drunk by three in the afternoon that I passed out in my backyard and didn't go pick up my sons from school. Not that I probably could have driven there to get them if I had been conscious. I think it's bullshit that all I ever wanted to be in life was a wife and mother, and given a hundred more chances, I couldn't possibly fuck either of them up any more royally than I did. That I wouldn't have left my kids' bedsides for a drink of water when they were sick and now I don't even live with them. Their father wouldn't even bring them here to see me on Family Day and there wasn't a damn thing I could do about it. That's total bullshit. I'm not blaming anyone else. I don't hear Mandy blaming anyone else." Jorie motioned to her friend. "It's not bullshit to care about the people we hurt."

Jorie didn't know if she was done talking, and apparently neither did anyone else in the group. They all sat in silence for what felt like hours, taking in what their quietest member had vented so passionately after three weeks of utter silence. Tara finally interrupted the still, quiet group.

"I think that's a good place to stop for today, everyone," she said.

News of Jorie's long-awaited contribution to her group meeting traveled fast. By the time she met with her counselor for their individual session later that afternoon, Debbie had been filled in on all the details. Jorie didn't understand what all the fuss was about really. All she did was say what was on her mind. Isn't that what they were supposed to be doing here?

"I know you don't think it's a big deal," Debbie began, "but Jorie, it is. Not the fact that you spoke in group. That's good, don't get me wrong. It's what you said."

Jorie glanced around the room, looking as though the meaning behind those words would be written on a pillow, a framed degree, or on the far wall. She didn't know what Debbie was getting at. "So what, I care about what people think about me. I didn't realize other people didn't care about that. Except maybe Phil."

"How much did you care about what people thought when you were drinking? How much did you care about what people thought when you couldn't quit drinking long enough to stay sober for your son's band concert and stayed home to sleep it off instead?" Debbie asked, leaning forward with her notebook gripped in her hand, as though it might fly off on its own. "How much did you really care about anything when you had to decide between somebody you loved and the alcohol?"

Jorie laced her hands behind her neck and closed her eyes. "I didn't," she said quietly.

Debbie hit her notebook hard with her free hand, making a cracking noise that caused Jorie's eyes to fly open. "Exactly!"

Over the thoughts that raced through her head, she barely heard the rest of what the counselor was saying. When she was drinking, she never cared enough about what others were going to think to actually stop, or even slow down. Every time she did think about the consequences of her behavior, the booze and her affair, she wanted another drink. It was far easier to drown the problem than actually look at it. It was beginning to sink in now, and Jorie found herself more terrified than ever about having to leave the facility and return to her "other" life.

That's exactly what she had to face the next weekend as she was packing up her things to go home. Jorie didn't miss the irony that when she came into rehab there was almost nothing she would have done to be able to just get back in Bronx's truck and go back to his place. Now the idea petrified her as much as being left there alone just a month earlier. Fear seemed to be the feeling that was most dominant in her life these days. No matter where she was or what she was doing, there was fear. It was getting old.

"Need any help packing?" It was Tara. She peeked her head around the door to Jorie's room, a smile on her face. Jorie tried to force a smile back at her, but it didn't come off.

"Nope, I think I got it. I mean if you really think I'm ready to leave. You know, if you think I need more time here I could sign back up, re-enlist, whatever you call it," Jorie said.

Tara chuckled. "I bet when you came in here you didn't think you'd be offering to stick around any longer than you had to, huh?"

She was reading Jorie's mind. Tara walked into the room and Jorie sank down onto the bed. "No, I can honestly say that thought never occurred to me." Tara sat next to Jorie as she went on. "How did you know that?"

Tara, smile still on her face, shook her head. "I've been doing this a long time, Jorie. Seldom do people come in truly wanting to be here, but more often than not they don't know what to do when it's time to leave."

Jorie looked at her, a serious expression on her face. "I don't think I'm ready…" It came out as a sentence, but Tara recognized the question mark that was in there as well.

"You're ready," Tara said softly. She put a hand on Jorie's shoulder. "I know I didn't get to hear you talk much while you were here, but when I did what you said told me you were ready. I wish everyone got how this works as quickly as you did."

Jorie leaned forward and rubbed her hands together, a nervous gesture she had developed over the past few weeks. "I don't remember what I did to deal before this. What I was like before I started this whole mess."

Tara leaned forward just as Jorie did and looked her in the eyes. "You don't have to go back to that. Who you were before. No offense, but I'm sensing that person didn't deal with things as well as you think she did." Both women let out soft laughs. "You can start over as somebody with tools to deal with whatever you face. Healthy tools. You're going to do just fine. You just have to figure out who that woman is."

Jorie almost told her that was easy for her to say, but just then Bronx's voice floated into the room, chasing every thought from Jorie's brain as it so often had. She gave Tara a quick hug before the group counselor excused herself from the room. Then her eyes locked with the ocean-blue of Bronx's, and she fell into his arms. A shudder went through her entire body, and Jorie knew it was time to go home.

Walking into Bronx's apartment felt like visiting some meaningful place from her childhood that was about to be torn down. She couldn't put her finger on it, but there was something about it that made her feel sad and out of place. Jorie wanted desperately to see her children when she got back to town, but it was so late that Ryan asked her to come by in the morning, rather than waking them. She was irritated that after a month without them he couldn't let them forsake a little sleep so that she could just hug each of them. But Jorie wasn't in a position to negotiate, so she agreed to come by first thing the next day.

"Rhea brought you a gift. It's on the table," Bronx told her as he walked to the bedroom with her bags.

Jorie pulled the card from the floral gift bag and smiled as she recognized her sponsor's handwriting on the envelope. She had written, 'Just because you're out doesn't mean you're alone. 7pm meeting tomorrow…I'll pick you up.' Jorie laughed and shook her head as she looked at the lotions and scented candles in the bag.

"Are you tired?" Bronx asked, coming up behind her but keeping his distance.

Jorie didn't know if she appreciated or resented his attempt to respect her space. She realized he didn't know how to act any more than she did, and that feeling of sadness swept over her again. What she really wanted was a glass of wine, but that obviously wasn't going to happen. Instead she did the only thing that had made her feel good any time in recent memory. She slid her arms around Bronx's neck. "Not really. You?"

He relaxed as he put his arms around her. "I could stay up for a while," he teased.

Jorie didn't feel that same rush following him to his bedroom as she had so many times before in their relationship. And despite her desire for a drink, she knew that wasn't the problem either. Something seemed to be missing, changed. After weeks of thinking and thinking in rehab, Jorie decided she would, just for that night, enjoy not having to think things through so hard. Whatever was different, she would just have to figure it out some other time.

* * * * *

She didn't wait for him to wake up the next morning before she scribbled a note and ran out the door. Jorie rang the doorbell at her own home, shifting her weight from foot to foot and feverishly rubbing her hands together. She saw Ryan's head peak around the curtain in the front window to see who it was, then he slowly unlocked the door, still in his pajamas.

"Good morning," he grumbled, looking as disheveled as she'd seen him in some time. "Little early, isn't it?"

Jorie knew when she was in the rehab center that she had no leverage with Ryan, but now that she was out the anger that had been growing in her became stronger. She wasn't waiting one more minute to see her children, and there wasn't anything Ryan was going to do to stop her this time.

She stepped into the front entryway. "Yeah, it is early. But since you never brought the kids to see me and didn't want me coming by last night, I thought I could be here this morning when they woke up. Unless you had some plans to try to stop me from doing that too?" She added sarcastically.

Ryan shook his head, too defeated to argue with her. He waved her in with his arms. "No, whatever. Come on in. They're all still in bed. Wake them, wait 'til they get up, I don't care." And with that he shuffled into the kitchen to make coffee. Jorie felt a bit disappointed that he was depriving her of the good fight she'd be preparing for since the snub on Family Day. She decided it could wait until another time. Right then there was nothing she wanted more than to see her kids.

Jorie spent the morning hearing everything Brennan and Grace had done over the past month, from field trips to catching a praying mantis in the backyard to basketball and ballet. Even the things they'd told her about during their frequent phone calls needed to be repeated, as though the stories were that much more interesting when told in person. They bounced as they talked, trying to yell over each other and battle for her undivided attention. They both wanted to be on her lap, both wanted to talk first and neither seemed willing to leave her side even when Ryan announced that he'd made bacon and eggs. Jorie finally convinced them to get washed up for breakfast with the promise that yes, she would sit right in between them so they could both be next to her. As they raced off to the bathroom, Jorie moved over on the couch next to Jack. He had hardly said a word to her since coming down from his bedroom.

"Jack," she began softly, "how have you been, honey?" She didn't know how to talk to him. Her son had become somebody she barely knew. Jorie wanted to put her arm around him, but he looked like he might run right out of the room if she did so.

"Fine," he mumbled.

Jorie risked putting her hand on his leg. He tensed up, but began to relax as she talked. "I guess you're pretty mad at me right now?"

Jack shook his head, his long hair falling in his eyes. "I'm not mad at anyone," he said in such a low tone Jorie could barely hear him. He wasn't very convincing.

"Really? Is that why you're not talking to me?"

"What do you want to talk about?" he asked sharply, looking at her for the first time that morning.

Jorie hadn't considered that he might react this way to her. She could see by Jack's face and demeanor that he would rather be almost anywhere else at that moment, and it felt like shards of glass hitting her heart. With one deep breath she silently asked God to give her the words that would help her son.

"Well, you know that I didn't leave you because I wanted to, right? Mom was sick, but I'm getting better, and I had to go away to do that. Do you understand that?" Jorie searched the boy's face for a sign that he wasn't as mad as he appeared. She could see that he was struggling, not wanting to be so angry at his mother but unsure how to forgive her.

"Yeah, whatever," he finally stammered. Jack moved to get up. "Can we go eat now?"

Jorie wanted to stop him, to explain herself further and make him understand the things that had happened to their family. But when she opened her mouth to begin speaking, she realized she didn't know herself. If she didn't understand it, how did she think a twelve year-old would?

After a breakfast full of more animated chatter from her two youngest children, Jorie helped clear the breakfast dishes with Ryan. She wanted a minute to talk to him in private about taking the kids for the day, maybe to the zoo or the park. It felt very odd, asking permission to spend time with her kids. The anger she had walked in the door with seemed to have dissipated during breakfast. Even in her resentment with Ryan about not bringing the kids to visit her, Jorie had profound guilt for having left him with all the responsibility of raising their three children. Not just while she was in rehab or living with Bronx, but really for the better part of the past few years. With her head clear of the alcoholic fog, it was almost blinding in its apparency that even though her kids loved her (at least Brennan and Grace did at that moment), Ryan really was their primary caregiver. She wanted desperately to change that, but right then the best thing she could do was give him the respect of recognizing the situation for what it was.

Ryan sighed deeply as he picked up the stopper for the sink and began running the water. He shook his head and said, "I don't know, it's your first day back. Are you really up for it?"

Jorie took the tone in his voice more as concern for the children more so than any real concern for her mental state or welfare. She bit her lip, fighting back resentment at the implication that she couldn't manage one day out with her own children. She tried to remind herself that his mistrust was something she had created on her own, and forced a tight smile.

"I get it. You're worried about them. But we need this time together. They need it and I need it." She tried to catch his eye. "I know I haven't garnered a lot of trust from you in the recent past, but you know I love my kids. I have screwed things up and all I want is a chance to try to fix it." Jorie had many more thoughts swirling in her head, most of which she knew would just make Ryan defensive and start a fight. She stopped talking and waited for his response.

He didn't look convinced, but conceded that they all probably needed a break. Jorie got the kids ready and headed out the door. She glanced back at Ryan, who looked fairly lost and lonely standing alone in the foyer of their house. It was the first time since she moved out that Jorie really felt the separation of their family, and that the connection between herself and her husband was completely severed.

Fifteen

AFTER A MONTH OF DAILY visits with the kids, some of which included Jack even speaking to her like a person, Jorie saw a note on the bulletin board at her afternoon meeting that caught her attention. She flicked the corner of it several times with her fingernail, considered taking it down, changing her mind over and over. After almost a full minute of staring at the flyer she pulled it out from under the push pin that held it up and gripped it in both hands. It was for a house rental.

"Deon," she said, walking up to the tall man working behind the coffee bar, "do you know this guy, Justin D?" She held the rental flyer up for him to see.

"Sure, I know Justin. He's a good guy. Good landlord. I rented one of his places when I first got clean. Takes real good care of his properties and his tenants. You lookin' for a place to rent?" Deon asked as he grabbed a Diet Coke out of the fridge without waiting for her to ask for it.

Jorie looked at the flyer quietly as she sat on one of the high stools, then began nodding her head. "Maybe, yeah. I mean, I need a place with more room for my kids. The place I'm staying now…" She put three quarters on the counter for the soda. "I love it, but it's not a place I can have the kids, you know?"

"Gotcha," Deon said. "Well I would definitely call him then," he added, tapping the flyer for emphasis.

That night after supper, Jorie set the flier in front of Bronx. "What's this?" he asked, looking it over quickly and then up at Jorie.

"I picked it up at my meeting today." She wasn't sure what to follow that up with. Most of the afternoon she'd spent just worrying about even bringing it up, never mind what she was actually going to say. She drew a blank.

Bronx seemed to be reading it over, then he looked at Jorie again, the same confused expression on his face. "I'm not sure where you're going with this. You know you have a home here. You don't have to go rent something."

"That's the thing, I do." Now the thoughts came to her faster. She sat down next to him and put a hand on his arm. "You've been awesome to let me stay here, but this is your home. I need to have a place where I can live with my kids."

"Do you think that's a good idea right now?" he asked. When he saw her eyes narrow in anger, he quickly finished with, "not that I don't think you can handle it. I just thought you weren't supposed to make any significant changes in your life in the first year after you got clean. I mean, isn't that what they say?"

Jorie didn't look any less irritated with his attempt at explaining his doubt. "I don't think being a mother to my children should be considered a 'significant change.' Do you?" she asked coolly.

"No, that's not what I was saying..." he started. Dodging bullets like this was becoming par for the course since Jorie got out of rehab, and Bronx was used to getting grazed from time to time. He knew there wasn't going to be an easy way out of this conversation. He sighed deeply and continued. "I think you should do what you need to do. You know I just don't want you to go." He took her hand and realized she was trembling. "Is that all this is about?" he questioned, trying to catch her eye.

Jorie looked away for a second, then brought her gaze up to meet his. She knew that wasn't all it was about, but any words that could follow a 'no' answer seemed to get caught in her throat, so she softly said yes. Bronx looked unconvinced, but was not willing to push her at that point.

"I'll help you check it out tomorrow, if you want."

"I, um," she began, stumbling on the words. "I already rented it."

"Oh," Bronx said simply, sitting back in his chair hard and looking a bit stunned. Jorie watched his face to see what the reaction would be, knowing full well it would be fine. She was so accustomed to the drama of what she was, mostly sarcastically, referring to as her former life it was hard to adjust to being able to just make decisions without the battle.

Jorie squeezed his hand, now trying to catch his eye. He looked at her, and the sadness in his eyes took her aback for a moment. "You know this isn't about us, right?" she questioned, her eyebrows raised. At that point, she wasn't sure if he did know that. She wasn't even sure if she knew it. He blinked slowly and nodded as she continued. "I have created this huge mess for my kids, and I *have* to do something about it. Sooner rather than later. I know you understand why I have to do this."

Bronx seemed to come out of the temporary shocked state he was in and looked at her more clearly now. "Yeah, yeah," he said, nodding quickly. "I get it. Do what you gotta do."

Jorie could tell he was as unconvinced as she was that either of them knew what the hell was going on, what to do, or what to say. Through her treatment she had learned that when you didn't know what to do or where to move, just stop. Be still. It was o.k. to just do nothing. Jorie hadn't stopped moving in three years, usually in the wrong direction. She wasn't good at immobility, but she was trying. This seemed like good training.

Despite his initial unstated apprehension and true to form, Bronx helped Jorie move into her new place the next weekend. She didn't have much to move, but had used some of her savings to buy furniture for the kids' rooms and the living room. She had expected a fight with Ryan over her request for increased time with their three children, but was pleasantly surprised at his willingness to give it to her. She could only guess he was somewhat relieved that she was no longer living at Bronx's loft, and thought that he probably welcomed some help with the parenting duties he'd undertaken almost exclusively over the past few months. Whatever the reason, Jorie didn't question it. Since they had done nothing formally on paper, she had very little leverage when it came to the kids. Certainly she didn't want to have to stand in front of a judge and argue that her children should be taken away from their dad, out of the only home they'd ever known. And for what, to be placed with Jorie in her rented house, barely months out of rehab following years of abusing alcohol, ignoring her family and cheating on her husband? That certainly sounded like fun. Maybe she could get the transcripts and frame it to hang over her dining table?

Drawing on the courage she'd gained from moving out of Bronx's and gaining more time with her kids, Jorie went back to her old decorating firm. She didn't know if they would be willing to take her back, or even if they'd have work for her, but decorating was the only thing she'd ever really loved doing. With bills to pay and kids to feed several days a week now, Jorie was worried that her money would run out much faster than it had been. She needed desperately to be somewhere, to have something meaningful to do with her time while the kids were in school and between meetings. Though Jorie wasn't sure what their response would be, she felt she'd developed enough of a reputation that if they didn't want her, another firm would. To her surprise, they were not only thrilled to have her back, but had work for her to start on right away. Jorie smiled as she set herself back up at the desk she'd occupied full-time before staying home to raise her kids. She knew that for the guys counting the money, hiring her back was a good financial move. For everyone else, they were just hoping for more drama and office gossip. Jorie chuckled softly. If only they knew how mellow her life had become in the midst of her 12-step work, maybe they wouldn't have been so eager to take her back.

Several weeks into a hotel restoration Jorie was part of, the project manager came up to her desk near the end of the day. "Got your kids tonight, Jorie?"

"Nope, they're with Ryan. Why?"

"We're all going over to the Maven. To celebrate." He noticed the look of confusion on Jorie's face. "The 171 account. We're going to be redoing all of their offices in the downtown building. Didn't you hear?"

Jorie shook her head. "No, I hadn't heard. That's great news, but I'm going to have to pass on the Maven." Jorie used to love going there for drinks with her eclectic group of co-workers, but that was before.

"Really?" Davis, who had been with the firm since Jorie was in high school, raised an eyebrow. "You might want to reconsider. I've heard the MG's are considering putting you on as the project manager. This is a huge account with a huge client. Big bucks," he said, emphasizing the word bucks with a sharp nod of his head.

Jorie's mind began to race. There was a time when she would have jumped at the opportunity to have a few drinks with her colleagues, and the idea of schmoozing with the big bosses for the chance to head up a major project like this would have been an even bigger draw. But Jorie had avoided any encounters that involved alcohol ever since getting out of rehab. She had missed birthday parties, barbeques and even a friend's wedding just so she wouldn't have to put herself in the position of having to say no to a drink. Much the same as she had done following her bariatric surgery, Jorie tried to avoid temptation. That was different. She quickly realized that no matter what her brain or her mouth said, her stomach wasn't going to allow her to eat too much. Drinking was an altogether different animal. It was all going to be up to her, and even one sip was going to be too much.

"Let me see, maybe I can work something out," Jorie said smiling. As soon as Davis left her office, she picked up the phone.

"You have to be able to live and function in the world, Jorie. But this is really about how comfortable you are with it. You haven't been dry very long. It's OK to just pass this time." Rhea's voice came calmly over the line.

Jorie sighed and said, "Yeah, I tried that. But if going to this thing gives me a better shot at managing a huge project like this, it would be stupid to turn it down. It's a huge opportunity, and geez I could use the money."

"More than you could use sobriety?"

Jorie sighed again, put her hand behind her neck and lowered her head. "Can't you just come with me?"

"Come with you?" Rhea asked as though she hadn't heard her right. "What am I going to do there? I can't keep you from drinking if you're going to drink."

"I'm not going to drink," Jorie said quickly. "I just think I would be a lot more comfortable around everyone else drinking if you were there. You know, as my support system."

"Like AA on tour? Maybe I could start a traveling company going around helping other recovering drunks attend work meetings, holiday parties and sporting events? Maybe get a tour bus?" Jorie shook her head at Rhea's sarcasm, but she could tell by the smile in her voice that her friend and sponsor would in fact come with her to give her the strength she needed.

When Jorie arrived home four hours later, she was emotionally exhausted. Going out had never been so much work. Even with Rhea there, being around all the beers, wines and mixed drinks made her mind spin. She had paced nervously from table to table, never staying in one place long enough for anyone to notice she didn't have a glass of wine or offer to buy her one. For the most part she was successful, until one of the company's owners asked her sit down and talk about the 171 account. He asked her repeatedly what he could get her to drink, made suggestions and at one point even ordered her the same thing he was drinking, a Black Russian. After her many failed attempts to pass him off with a simple 'no, thank you,' Jorie looked him squarely in the eye and said as firmly and respectfully as she could muster, "Thank you, but I *don't* drink!" Rhea overheard it and looked up from her conversation with a designer who was giving her tips for getting her house organized (good luck with that one, Jorie thought). She smiled at Jorie, kept an eye on her for a minute as if gauging whether she needed help, and then returned to her closet and cabinet discussion. Her boss also looked at Jorie quizzically for a minute, and then went on talking about the new business account as if she'd never said a thing. And he never offered her another drink the rest of the night.

Though Jorie was pleased with her decisions from the evening, it wasn't an experience she want to have again anytime soon.

The next morning her doorbell rang just as she finished making coffee. Jorie was a bit surprised to see Bronx standing on her patio with a beautiful bouquet of flowers. She broke into a huge smile.

"I haven't seen you all week, so I didn't want to show up empty handed," he said with a slanted grin.

Jorie stepped to the side so he could come in. She hadn't realized until he had said it that they *hadn't* seen each other all week. It was the longest they had gone without spending at least some time together for as long as she could remember. Not long ago she hadn't been able to make it through one or two days apart from him without it sending her into a wine-induced coma. Now she had her own place and nobody to answer to, but had made no real effort to get together with him. The thought made her face flush.

"Are you feeling alright?" he asked when he saw the blush color cross her features.

"Yeah, I'll be fine," she said. Jorie pushed the concern back down that was creeping up in her stomach. She reached one hand behind his neck and gave him a soft kiss. "Do you want some coffee?"

"Not really," he said in a low, deep voice, keeping his eyes on hers as he reached over and put the flowers on the table. Once he had wrapped his arms around her waist and she could smell his cologne on the collar of his t-shirt, Jorie convinced herself that she was reading too much into their week apart. She had been working hard, and Bronx had begun working for himself doing independent electrical jobs. They were both just busy. It was alright.

After spending the morning in bed together, Jorie was reluctant to get up and get ready for the day. She could have laid there in his arms for the rest of her life and exited this world happy. Her earlier apprehension buried, she leaned up on her elbow and looked at his unshaven face.

"Let's go somewhere."

Bronx reached up and pushed away a stray bang that had fallen across Jorie's face. "OK, where do you want to go?"

"I don't know, somewhere warm. With a beach. I've always wanted to go to the beach. I might be put in charge of this big job we have coming up, and even if I'm not the project manager it will still be a ton of work for all of us, so we should go before it gets started."

"Hey, that's great about the job," he said, looking at her more intently. "When did that come up?"

Jorie just realized she hadn't even told him about her night out with the company or the biggest design job her firm had ever worked on. An unexplained disquiet filled her head again, and this time she could feel herself mentally shoving it out of the way. "Oh, just something we found out about this week. So where are we going to go? Mexico? The Caribbean?"

"Anywhere you are sounds good to me." Bronx's stunning blue eyes focused on her in that way that always made her skin tighten and tingle. "I can work on it today. Don't you have to go to a meeting with Rhea?"

"Oh shit, I gotta get ready," Jorie murmured, glancing at the clock as she threw her covers off.

Jorie was excited for this meeting. She was getting her six month chip. It had felt like the longest six months of her life, but she figured that was probably because it was the first stretch of time she could remember in quite a while!

When Jorie saw Bronx later in the week he had come up with a plan for their trip. She had two days to get ready for it, and she spent most of it tearing apart her closet looking for the right clothes to bring. Even years after her weight-loss surgery, Jorie's wardrobe ranged within four sizes. She had never been so thin in her adult life, but yet couldn't bring herself to get rid of some of her larger clothes. That was a bad idea…too much wiggle room if one really wanted to start overeating again. Now that she was off her cocktail breakfasts, lunches and dinners, Jorie knew that was a definite possibility. It gave her that much more determination to stay at both her AA and OA meetings.

After having determined that none of the items in her closet would do for the trip, Jorie decided to check one last place before she was willing to give up and buy some new clothes at the mall down the road. In a large box she'd brought over from the house during the move was a laundry hamper which had a whole pile of clothes she hadn't looked at for quite a while. She almost didn't open it, thinking to herself how crazy it was to not just buy something new. This was a special occasion, after all. And money wasn't nearly as tight anymore.

A minute later, Jorie was sitting on the floor immobile. Digging through the pile of laundered clothes she found a t-shirt and pair of sweats she had worn at her highest weight. They were extra big, because she always wanted to be comfortable and rarely went anywhere anyway. As she held the pants up to her waist, she realized she could have fit her new body into them at least three times. The t-shirt was so big it probably could have fit her whole family *and* Bronx in it. That image made her smile slightly, but it didn't last. She reached back into the hamper to see what other nightmare ensembles she would come out with, but instead of clothing pulled out a half-empty bottle of vodka.

As Jorie sat against the wall and slid down to the floor, she couldn't take her eyes off the bottle. She had seen this moment in movies before. OK, she was supposed to have an internal struggle over this. If she drank it, she would be right back in the same boat she'd basically fallen out of six months ago. If she drank it, all the things she'd worked so hard to reestablish over the past few months would be gone. Again. If she drank it, she could really lose her kids for good, would probably be unemployed and God only knew what else. Because if she drank it, she couldn't stop at just that bottle.

Jorie saw the clothes she'd just been chuckling over come into focus behind the bottle. How in the hell did her life get to be such a mess? Where exactly had she managed to take a fairly intelligent, sweet young girl and turn her into the larger-than-life (literally), incredible shrinking, adulterous, selfish boozehound mother and wife from hell? At what point did the excesses that she had so willingly indulged in become who she was?

The bottle flew back in the box as though it was on fire. Jorie tossed the old, oversized clothes in on top, slammed the box top shut and carried it out to the large black garbage can sitting on the berm, waiting for the weekly trash pickup. She looked down the street towards a diesel sound to see that the garbage truck was nearly to her house. Jorie smiled as she climbed into her car and headed out of the driveway towards the mall.

* * * * *

Sitting on the plane, Jorie felt a peace she hadn't had in a while. Maybe it was a combination of being with Bronx, whom she'd seen so little of in the recent past. Maybe it was being headed for a destination she had dreamed about visiting for such a long time. Jorie didn't know why people always complained about how cramped airline seats were. She thought it was plenty roomy, but couldn't have imagined feeling that way before her surgery. She was tucked in just snuggly enough against Bronx, and it gave her a calm to feel his warm arm against hers.

"How ya doing?" Bronx asked as he nuzzled her ear with his nose.

Jorie shook her head and smiled. "Awesome," she breathed. When she looked at him, the cool blue of his eyes made her stomach jump just as it had at the beginning of their relationship. It occurred to her that it had been some time since that feeling registered in her body, and it was comforting to have it back. When he took her hand, her skin felt hot. It was so much like it had been in the beginning; Jorie closed her eyes and sank back into her seat. She had not been so contented in ages.

Their entire week went as well as the plane ride. First thing after checking into the hotel, Jorie excitedly changed into her new swimsuit (she still couldn't believe she'd actually bought one) and bolted for the beach. They swam in the bath warm waters, laid out on huge fluffy towels, wrote their names in the sand and took pictures of it. Jorie wanted to avoid the bars that lined the beach under huge straw awnings, so Bronx brought her sodas, waters and pink fruity shakes with little umbrellas. Though Jorie had a passing feeling of guilt that she had never taken Ryan up on his offer to bring her on one of these vacations when they were together, she knew it never would have felt the same to her as being there with Bronx.

The last night they were on the island, they were taking a walk on the beach. Jorie thought the warm fresh air and sound of the surf was too perfect to fully comprehend. She leaned her head against Bronx's strong shoulder and took a deep breath. He suddenly stopped walking.

"Did you see that falling star?" He pointed up into the dark sky over the water.

Jorie cocked her head and looked in that direction. "All I see is that airplane," she commented about the small blinking light in the distant sky. "Did you make a wish?"

Bronx turned to face Jorie and pulled a box out of the pocket of his pants. "Yes I did. Let's see if it will come true."

Jorie looked down as the lid of the box rose and saw the most stunning antique ring set with several sapphires and a large diamond in the center. It caught the moonlight just right and sparkled as if it were under the display lights in a jewelry store. She put her hand up to gingerly touch the exquisite ring, then looked up at Bronx.

"I'm probably not going to get this out quite right," he stammered. Jorie automatically grinned at his usual humble charm, as tears began to fill the corners of her eyes. "I know you're still trying to get things back on track. But I can't imagine not being a part of your life. I always want you to be part of mine." Bronx lifted the ring out of the box and Jorie held up her left hand. As he slid the ring on her finger, he smiled nervously. "You're letting me put it on. Is that a yes?"

Jorie began nodding, first slowly and then more fervently. "Yes, it's definitely a yes," she whispered. She threw her arms around his neck.

The next day as they boarded the plane to return home, Jorie caught a glimpse of the beautiful ring that adorned her left hand. She smiled at the sparkle that ricocheted off the edge of the diamond, and then burst out laughing.

Bronx looked at her with a grin. "What?"

Jorie stifled her laugh and shook her head. "Oh nothing," she said, shrugging off the question. She was too embarrassed to admit that it just occurred to her; she probably ought to get divorced from her first husband before she married a new one.

Sixteen

THE NEXT FEW WEEKS PASSED so quickly Jorie felt as if she were in a wind tunnel. Being project manager was something she had dreamed of doing for years at her firm, and now realized what an overwhelming task it could be. The day after returning from her incredible dream vacation, she found an attorney to start divorce proceedings. Her conversation with Ryan about that went much better than Jorie could have anticipated. He hadn't warmed to her much in the year they'd been separated, but he'd never filed for divorce either. She knew there was always going to be a hope in his mind that they would reconcile, that she would "come to her senses" and that he might eventually find a way to forgive her for having an affair. Jorie was not sure if it was the passing of time or the ring on her finger that made him concede that was a very unlikely probability. She didn't have time to figure out what it was. She barely had time for the meeting with the attorney.

"So, what? Do we need to figure out what to do with the stuff around here? You can take whatever you need." Ryan said wearily as they sat on the couch in what Jorie used to think of as their family room. She had a hard time thinking of it as that anymore.

"I think I'm alright. I got all my stuff out when I moved into my house." As she looked around, Jorie realized she wouldn't want anything from their home in her new place. The guilt was draped on the furniture like a crocheted afghan from a long-dead relative. She couldn't look at that every day. It made her suddenly saddened that Ryan did, shuffling around that big empty house all alone on the days she had the kids. No wonder he was having such a hard time letting go.

Jorie forced herself to continue what she'd come over to talk to him about. "Um, I don't think we're going to have too much to deal with as far as separating property. What I guess we should discuss is the kids." She paused, waiting for his reaction. There was none. "Ryan, I know you've taken care of them by yourself since…" Jorie stopped, realizing *that* wasn't going to be the best thing to mention during this conversation. "And I don't want to uproot them anymore than they've already been. But they're my kids. I can't just give them up in a divorce, like furniture or dishes. They should be with both of us."

Ryan snapped a look at Jorie when she said that. "Yes, they should," he said coldly.

Jorie forced a civil voice, even managing to soften her tone. "What I mean is that I think we should share custody. I know it's not ideal. I'm sure we'd both just love to have them all the time. But that's just not possible right now."

"Actually it is possible," Ryan nodded, looking at her poignantly. He had the biggest, most cheerless brown eyes when he looked at her, and Jorie felt like she was looking at the face of a person dealing with the grief of just being informed a loved one had died. She squirmed on the sofa. She had seen a friend in rehab receive the news that her son had been killed in a car crash, and she had felt at least as uncomfortable then. She knew what stage was next and dreaded it.

"Ryan, are you going to fight me on this? I just want equal time with the kids. I know I've been a crappy mother to them the last few years, but I'm the only mother they have and I'm coming out of this stronger. You know they're my whole world. Please don't make us all go through a battle."

Jorie thought for a moment that Ryan was going to launch into one of his speeches about how he wasn't the one making them go through all this, how it wasn't his screw-up that was causing all the problems. She braced herself for it, but it never came.

"Alright," he agreed. "Have your lawyer draw up whatever papers he needs to and I'll sign them."

She was shocked, but quickly felt compelled to get out of that room, and out of that house. She stood up a little too sharply, then looked again at Ryan with the most compassion she had felt for him in some time. "Thank you," she said simply and made her way to the door. Whatever the next stage of grief was that Ryan would experience, she didn't want to be there to see it.

As Jorie threw herself into the task of managing a major redecorating project, she found herself overwhelmed with all the work she had to do, finding time to spend with her kids and Bronx, and making all her meetings. After a few months, her divorce from Ryan was final. He had been as agreeable through the rest of the process as he was the day she first broached the subject with him. Jorie was constantly on edge, just waiting for him to lose his cool, flip out at meeting with the attorneys, or decide to fight her for full custody after all. It never happened, and in the end she was surprised that she had even questioned how he would behave. It was her actions that had been so out of character for the past few years. Ryan had always been Ryan…the same sweet, soft-hearted young man she had married. Even the shit she put him through couldn't drive that out of him, and she found a new admiration for him as a man, even if she couldn't find her passion for him anymore.

"So, this seems like the best time to bring this up," began Bronx as they were having sushi the weekend after she received the final decree from the courts. "I'd like to know what you were thinking about for a wedding? Big, small, when? That kind of thing. Got any ideas?"

Jorie had anticipated these questions were coming, but she didn't know the answers to any of them. The truth was, she really hadn't thought much about her marriage to Bronx. The term even sounded weird to her. Their relationship had been so different and separate from her first "marriage," so thinking of Bronx as her husband seemed somehow off to Jorie. She didn't want to think that way. When he looked at her intently as he was just then, those sky-colored eyes boring into her very being, she couldn't imagine herself spending life any other way. Still, there was some sort of mental block keeping her from acknowledging that he was, indeed, going to be her husband.

She spun the ring on her left hand around her finger, a habit she's picked up years earlier. Jorie smiled to herself as she realized how long it had been since she'd actually done it. She had stopped wearing her wedding band from Ryan shortly after all her weight loss. She told him it didn't fit, though what she didn't explain was that she meant that as figuratively as she did physically. It had been years since she'd had a ring on that finger, and though Bronx had obviously bought this one in her current size, it somehow didn't seem to fit either.

"I don't know," she smiled at him and cocked her head to the side. "Small I guess. I think big second marriages are a kind of tacky. What were you thinking?"

"It really doesn't matter to me. Small is fine. As long as you're my wife, I don't care how many people are there or how we do it."

Jorie looked over at the windows of the restaurant, not able to meet his tender gaze. "Well, I guess it will have to be in the summer, or over a school break so the kids can be there." She looked over at Bronx and caught his look of surprise. "What, you didn't think the kids would be there?"

"No, of course they'll be there. I guess that's why you're the mom. When kids are in school is not something I would think to consider. But either summer or during a break, that's fine with me."

Jorie couldn't control her unwarranted irritation. "Have you even thought through the fact that you're talking about being a step-dad? I mean, do you know what that means? You're not just getting a wife, but three other people to deal with. And Ryan is always going to be there too, in one way or another. Are you really sure that you want that?"

Bronx, his usual patience intact, took her hand. "Yes, I have thought of it. I think your kids are great. I know we don't know each other very well, but that's gonna change over time. My mind isn't programmed in 'kid-time' just yet, but it will come." Jorie just stared at him. "Are you alright? You seem a little on edge tonight," Bronx asked.

"I'm alright," Jorie responded, nodding slowly. She didn't know why she'd jumped down his throat like that, but she did know that she really wasn't in the mood to discuss wedding plans she hadn't had the time or motivation to make. "Just a stressful week, I guess."

They made small talk for the rest of the meal, but Jorie couldn't shake the idea that something was off with her. She wanted to be excited about planning a wedding, about planning her marriage. There was a time in her life she couldn't get through the day without a drink because being away from Bronx felt too hard. Now she had the opportunity to spend her whole life with him, without the guilt of cheating on her husband and neglecting her family, and she couldn't get into it. She started to wonder when and why her thinking had become so scrambled?

"You're an addict," was Rhea's matter-of-fact response when Jorie brought up the question at their meeting that week. "If your thinking wasn't so fucked up, maybe you wouldn't have to use food or alcohol to cope. Or maybe if you didn't use those things your thinking wouldn't be so fucked up. Either way, you're an addict. You know what you have to do about it. That's all you can do is the next right thing."

Jorie looked at her thoughtfully. "But I don't want to be like that anymore."

Rhea laughed right out loud, causing several people in the coffee shop they were seated in to look over in their direction. "Well hell

Jor, why didn't you say so? Let me just run out to my car and grab my magic wand. We'll fix you right up."

Jorie rolled her eyes. "You know what I mean."

"Oh, I know exactly what you mean," Rhea said, without the sarcasm. "You want to feel like you're normal, whatever the hell that is. We all want to feel like that, but you're not normal. Neither am I. We just have to deal with life the way it comes, so if that means making hard decisions rather than ignoring them and climbing into a bottle, that's what we do. If we don't, we die. Maybe not physically at first, but spiritually and emotionally and eventually our body goes too."

"So what are you saying, just suck it up?"

"No," Rhea said with a chuckle, "I'm saying do the work. You know what you need to do. You're not even through the steps in AA yet. I know they're the same steps as OA but you weren't sober when you did those. Do you really think you did them as thoroughly as you would do them now?"

Jorie shook her head.

Rhea pushed on. "They say not to make any big changes in your first year, but you've had to make some. Tough ones and big ones and scary ones, but they couldn't be avoided. I'm just saying that the changes you have control over should wait until you've been dry longer. You have to decide what those changes are and put them on the back burner. Does that make sense?"

Jorie swallowed the lump in her throat as she nodded. She didn't dare say anything for fear that she was going to burst into tears. Rhea read the look of pain on her friend's face.

"I'm not saying don't marry him, Jorie," Rhea said in a low, soft tone. "I've sponsored a LOT of people in my years in program and I've never seen anyone stand by somebody the way he does you. You know what I think of him. Despite the way you guys started out, I don't think I've ever seen a more love-sick dog in my life." Both women laughed. "But you came to me with this, and I'm just trying to help you figure out what **you** need."

"I don't know what that is," Jorie said, her voice barely above a whisper.

"Then you know what to do," said Rhea simply.

Jorie did know what to do. She needed to pray. She needed to stay still. She needed to breathe...

She managed to avoid the wedding conversation over the next few weeks. Jorie was still swamped with managing her decorating project and sharing custody of the kids with Ryan. As things with work began to wind down, it was apparent she was going to have to make some plans for her new marriage.

"How about we just go back to Mexico to get married? Just the two of us?" she asked one night, sprawled on the bed in his loft where they had first made love. That seemed like so many eons ago now. Not just in another lifetime, but on another planet.

"What about the kids? I thought you wanted them to be there."

Jorie couldn't imagine starting a life with somebody without her kids to celebrate with her. But somehow it felt better to do it without them. It pained her that she would do such a sacred thing without them there. Maybe it was because she and Bronx had started out as such a contrast to what her marriage was supposed to mean. Maybe it was because she had a hard time seeing anyone but Ryan as a father-figure to them. Either way, Jorie felt like if she didn't bite the bullet and get on with some plans, this wedding might never take place. Not exactly the grand dreams of a bride-to-be, she realized, but a forward movement none the less.

"I just want us to be married. We can celebrate with them when we get back. They'll understand." Jorie felt guilty mentioning the deeper issue. Based on what the kids knew about their relationship, though it wasn't much, they weren't in a big hurry to be part of any celebration that saw their mother married to anyone but their father. She understood that, but didn't think sharing that with Bronx was going to set the right tone for their new life together as a family.

"OK," he said, "that one is your call. When do you want to go?"

"I have a week off coming up at the end of next month. I need to be here on the 29th to get my one year chip at my meeting, but maybe we could fly out the next day?"

Bronx sat up in bed and looked at her. "Jesus J, you're getting your chip! I didn't even realize it had been a whole year. That's great!" He had a look of excitement in his eyes that made Jorie's face flush with embarrassment. "We'll have two things to celebrate in Mexico."

Jorie was able to go to sleep with some peace that night. The first anniversary of her new life was coming up, and it felt somehow more real because of the excitement Bronx put into it. She was becoming more comfortable with their wedding plans, and things in her life hadn't looked so good in a long, long time. If only she could stop spinning that ring. No matter how she adjusted it on her finger, it never settled in the right place.

Seventeen

WHEN SOMEBODY AT HER AA meeting celebrated a birthday, they asked the person to get up and tell their story. At her OA meetings, people seemed to tell their stories all the time. Sometimes whole meetings would be taken up by a couple of their members sharing much of what had led them to believe they were addicted to food, and how their behavior had affected those around them. In AA, it was different. Sure, some members shared parts of their history and things they had been through. But mostly it was about the program, their recovery, and what they were doing to get better. Experience, strength and hope. Jorie thought about what she had been taught about picking a sponsor. "Find someone who has what you want, and ask them." She had heard that over and over again. Hearing about what people had been through was helpful, but hearing about how they were getting well had saved her life. She was looking forward to sharing her story, and was at the same time terrified of saying some of it out loud. What she wanted to do was be honest and real about what she had done, but also to give credence to the program that gave her back her sanity and ability to function in life.

During lunch with Rhea the day before her birthday meeting, Jorie discussed with her the problems she was having putting her feelings about what had gone on in her life into words. Rhea, in her usual uncomplicated manner, shook her head and looked at Jorie with a most adoring smile.

"Sweetie, it's your story. There is nothing I can tell you about how to tell it. But I can tell you that no matter how you say it, nobody in that room is going to think you did it wrong. Stop planning it out. When you get up there, your Higher Power is going to give you the words you need at the time. All you have to do is ask Him."

Jorie felt relief wash over her. She had developed a whole new relationship with this entity the people in her 12-step groups called a higher power. Though she was getting better about it, she recognized that when she was dealing with anything truly stressful, she often forgot to engage that relationship and talk to Him directly. She was so grateful to have Rhea as such a great reminder that she needed that connection with her Higher Power, and could have it any time she asked for it.

The feeling of anxiety returned briefly the next night as she sat in the room where she had spent so many hours over the past eleven months. Since getting out of rehab, Jorie had found what she considered her home group, and attended much of her meetings there. The people in her group had become like her family, and all of them had come out on this evening to see her pick up her chip and hear her tell her story. She knew there was no pressure to say the right thing, but it was hard not worry that she was going to be able to get through all of it without breaking down. Bronx, sensing her unease, took her hand.

"OK?" he asked, squeezing gently as he raised her hand to his lips and gave it the gentlest of kisses.

Jorie immediately relaxed, and smiled at him. "Yes, I am now."

When the introductions and general readings were done, Jorie took a deep breath, knowing her turn to speak was coming. George, one of the long-timers (as they were called) chaired the meeting, and he gave such an incredibly touching intro that she was almost in tears before she even made it to the podium at the front of the room. Over the past few years, she had developed such disdain for herself because of her actions; it was hard to wrap her mind around being cared for by so many people that she only knew from these rooms. It overwhelmed her at times to garner such unconditional love from people who all had some idea of the place she had come from and the things she had done. Though she was working on finding love for herself despite her many flaws, she always felt loved by the other people in her program, and some days that love was all that got her through.

Jorie gave George a big hug as she accepted the shiny gold coin with a Roman numeral I on it. As she turned it over in her hand, the metal felt cold and then warmed in her palm. She knew the tradition of the birthday meeting was to pass the coin around the room so that each member could say a silent prayer for her continued recovery. She wanted to honor that, but in that moment she couldn't let the solid disc out of her nervous grasp.

She approached the podium and began with a deep sigh, all the while asking her Higher Power to give her the right words to express how she felt, and if He meant for it, to help somebody else in the room that might be going through what she'd gone through. One thing Jorie had discovered over the past year was to never assume what others might be struggling with, or what she might say that could make a difference to somebody. It had happened to her just like that, more than once. Sometimes the people you think are the least like you can be the people who understand you the most. And sometimes the people you would never guess, have done or been through worse than you.

"I know I'm supposed to pass this," she began quietly, holding up the chip, "but I'm not sure I'm ready to let go of it just yet." There was soft laughter from the group. Those who were not AA members thought it was cute, but those who had been where she was understood it was more than cute. It was her lifeline in that moment, and they were all too happy to let her hold on to it as long as she needed to.

Jorie cleared her throat to reach the large group of people gathered in the meeting room. She started out stiffly, almost sounding like she were reading off a script. As she caught Rhea's eye, then Bronx's, she began to relax, and the words came more naturally. She talked about her childhood for a minute, her father's drinking and the way she learned to cope in high school with inadequacies, disappointments, and boys using alcohol. Though it was the turning point in her young life, she only briefly mentioned the accident that devastated her world when she was 20. She explained how becoming a wife and a mother had given her new goals and put things into perspective for her, but that she was already using food as a coping tool so she didn't need the booze anymore. Then came the part of her story she was dreading. It was the part that had filled her with the most brilliant inner light, while taking her soul to the darkest depths she could have ever imagined.

Jorie knew this was going to be the most difficult thing for her to talk about. She had mulled it over and over, and no matter how she looked at it, she couldn't truly tell her story without explaining that it was the guilt of her affair that lead her to start drinking again. Hard. It wasn't just the guilt, but the obsessive love she felt for Bronx, which itself was almost like a drug. Of course, she knew that she wasn't saying anything he didn't already know. But having him there, sitting and listening and hearing it come out of her mouth for the first time made her face flush hot and her heart rush. She couldn't look at him.

"When I realized I felt something for somebody who wasn't my husband," she began somberly, "I didn't know how to handle it. It was the only thing I wanted and the absolute last thing I should have had." Jorie settled a bit, seeing several people in the group nod their heads. She knew they may not have had affairs, but they were familiar with the sentiment. As usual, their empathy pushed her forward. "When I was drunk, I didn't have to think about all the things I was doing wrong. When I was with him, I didn't want anything else, but that feeling seemed so dreadfully wrong that I needed a drink to block it out. When I couldn't be with him, drinking was like sleeping. It seemed like the quickest way to get to the next high with him, and not really have to face the time in between. I...I..." Jorie stopped, choked on the words in her throat and glanced at Bronx. It was as if a bowling ball had hit her in the head. Like she had been punched, and cartoon images of stars swam before her eyes. She couldn't speak anymore. The revelation was so overpowering that all the words in the universe ceased to exist, and only awareness was left in their place.

"Jorie?" George asked quietly, touching her arm. She jumped, as if being woken up from a nightmare of falling, and she was back in the room. Back with all those faces staring at her, waiting for her to go on. She blushed again, and nodded at George that she could continue. There was more to say, but the strike she had received made it difficult to remember everything. Jorie stammered through the rest of her speech, making sure to thank Bronx for everything, her dear friends from her meetings and most especially Rhea, who had been the rock she needed on so many occasions. The days ahead were going to be even more telling of the strength of their relationship.

"Oh, I'm so proud of you!" Rhea gushed as she hugged Jorie after the meeting was ended with a prayer. "How are you doing? Are you good?" Jorie nodded, but pulled her friend in close enough to whisper in her ear. When Jorie was done, Rhea backed up and looked at her sponsee gravely. "Tomorrow then," she nodded, not taking her eyes off Jorie's.

Jorie didn't sleep that night. Bronx was disappointed that she went back to her place alone, but she explained that the emotion of the night had gotten to her, and that she needed to just have some quiet. Of course she could have had all the peace she wanted at his place, but it wasn't the same thing. She needed the isolation. She needed to think. She *still* needed to breathe.

"I can't do it, I can't. I just can't do it," Jorie rambled the next day at lunch with Rhea. She picked up a piece of the free bread the waitress had brought to the table, but she didn't eat it. She just nervously tore it into little pieces, tossing it on the small plate with a trembling hand.

Rhea leaned across the table. "What happened ,Jorie?"

"I can't marry him," Jorie said in a hoarse, quiet voice. She looked directly at Rhea. "I can't," she repeated as tears began spilling down her cheeks.

"OK," Rhea tried to reassure her, "it's OK. Nobody's saying you have to get married. Did something happen with Bronx?"

"No, well no, nothing really happened," she stuttered, fidgeting in her chair. She sat up, put her foot under her bottom, and then dropped it back to the ground. "I mean, nothing new really happened. I just, I don't KNOW what happened!" This came as almost a shout, and she tried to lower her voice. "Look, all I know is that when I was telling my story last night, all of a sudden it just hit me. It had been staring me in the face the whole time and I couldn't see it."

"I don't understand," Rhea shook her head.

Jorie looked at her intently. "This whole thing with us started out wrong. It couldn't have started out any more wrong if I tried. Every time I look at him, every time I sleep in that bed I think about what I did. Every time I stay there I want a drink more than any other time, in any other place. I just can't do it, Rhea. I can't marry him and stay sober!"

For the first time in their relationship as friends, confidantes and sponsor and sponsee, Rhea didn't know what to say. This scared the hell out of Jorie. Rhea always knew what to say. Even when she didn't have the answers to Jorie's problems, she still had something to say. Anything. She had never felt so defeated.

Jorie shook her head. "Even you don't have an answer to this one."

Despite Rhea's attempt to help her work through what seemed like an impossible predicament, Jorie left the restaurant feeling there could be no resolution that wouldn't break her heart in one way or another. All the hours in the world could be dedicated to weighing the pros and cons of what she must do and in the end, there was only one answer that was going to bring her the serenity she prayed for daily. Without that, Jorie didn't know what there could be for her in life.

She walked for an hour, not really thinking about where she was going. Something was guiding her, and she eventually found herself at the oldest park in town. When she was a child, Jorie's father would bring her down to play on the metal slide and swing on the huge suspended rubber tire, now cracked and worn with age. She hadn't been there in years, but it looked the same as she remembered. The same, except that everything seemed smaller. Jorie had been just a little bit the last time she'd sat on the rusty old merry-go-round, but somehow she felt smaller too. It pained her to think of that little girl, just starting to deal with the world in all the wrong ways. She wanted so much to talk to her then, to tell her that things didn't have to be so difficult. She wanted somebody to come tell her that very same thing right then, and that's when she looked up.

As the warm fall sun settled in behind a mass of inflated white clouds, the light spread out in beams of pale yellow, illuminating the glassy blue of the sky. In the colors Jorie could see Bronx's brilliant eyes, the flecks of silver that made them sparkle and her knees give out. She stood up slowly, then almost broke into a run all the way back to her car still parked at the restaurant. By the time she had driven to his loft, she felt there was little strength left in her muscles.

"Hey," he smiled as she walked in the front door. He was carrying a small suitcase and set it by the doorway. "Got your bag ready for tomorrow?" he asked cheerfully as he slid his hand around her waist.

Jorie resisted his advancing kiss by pushing back and ducking around him. She walked to the middle of his very tastefully decorated living room. The room she had decorated. The room where they had made love more times than she could count, and the room where she was about to trade her heart for her serenity.

"I didn't pack," Jorie began, her voice a murmur. She put her hands on the back of her neck and looked up at the vaulted ceiling. She inhaled deeply. Slowly she let the air out as she leveled her head to look at Bronx. He stared at her, unmoving.

"Jorie, what's going on?" His voice was low and hesitant.

She looked away for a second, unable to meet his intent stare. She owed it to him to look at him when she told him. That would be all the honor she could give their relationship in that moment.

"I didn't pack. I'm not going to Mexico because I can't marry you." She said it as firmly as she could muster, but her voice wavered and came dangerously close to cracking.

Bronx looked completely confused as he walked towards her. He shook his head gently, as though he were trying to adjust the information he had just received so it would fit in correctly. When he got within a few feet of her, Jorie took a step backwards. That made him stop in his tracks, and both eyebrows went up.

"I don't get it," he said, almost as though it were a question. "What do you mean you can't marry me? We're supposed to go to Cabo in the morning." He shook his head again. "What the hell is going on, J?"

The tears started, and Jorie couldn't stop them. But she did manage to control her emotions enough to be able to speak. She had always hated to cry, especially in front of anyone. But this time she knew there was going to be nothing she could do about it.

"I…I," she found herself stammering, much like she had at the end of her speech when she received her one year chip. Jorie was afraid she wasn't going to be able to get the words out, but she dug her fingernails into the palm of her hand to pull her out of the dizzying feeling that threatened to make her pass out. "I love you so much," Jorie said slowly. "I wish it didn't have to be this way. I just, I…we can't get married." Jorie reached down to her left hand and pulled off the striking ring he had given her several months earlier. She held out the ring towards him.

Bronx put both hand up in the air, this time backing up himself. "No," he said, shaking his head for the third time. "No, I'm not taking that back. Jorie," he looked at her fixedly, "I don't know what happened, but we'll work it out. If you need more time, we don't have to get married right now. Things have been really intense for you this year, but it doesn't mean…" He cocked his head to one side. "It doesn't mean *this*."

Jorie bordered on sobbing at this point. She continued to hold the ring out in Bronx's direction. He stayed back as though she were holding a knife towards him.

"It does have to mean this. Please, just take it," she pleaded through her tears.

Bronx still didn't move. "Jorie, can you please just tell me what happened? You can't just walk in and say we're not getting married and not tell me what the hell is going on. Did I do something?"

"No," Jorie said weakly, finally putting down her outstretched arm but still pinching the ring between her finger and her thumb. Now she was the one to shake her head. "You didn't do anything." She looked at the ring, then back at Bronx. "I know you want some kind of explanation here. I wish I had one for you." Her shoulders slumped, and she sunk into the closest chair.

Bronx walked over and crouched down in front of her. He lowered his head to catch her eye. "I don't think I get any of this. So we don't get married now, but what else does that mean? You can't tell me why?"

Jorie felt the desperation in his voice. He was grasping for anything from her, and she had nothing to give. All the times she had run out on him to get home, the night of his housewarming party where Ryan's speech was a painful reminder that she wasn't really his, even the fiasco at the barbeque; the combination of all that anguish didn't feel like a tenth of what she saw in his eyes right then. Bronx, whose even keel was one of his most enduring qualities, had the raw look of true despair across his face.

"I don't know how to explain this without causing more pain," she began, really looking at him for the first time.

"Just tell me what the problem is. We can figure it out."

"No," she broke down. "There is nothing to figure out. Nobody has ever treated me the way that you do. I know you deserve so much more than this. I just can't be that person for you. This just started out all wrong, and I don't know how to function in this with you. Without a drink." She paused and looked at him intently. "I know how weak that makes me sound. But when I'm here, with you, it's like that's the only thing I can think about."

"So I'll move…" Bronx started. "I don't have to live here. If it's this place, that's fixable."

"It's not just this place. It's everything about us. When I look at you, it just reminds me of all the mistakes I've made and what I haven't been to my kids, and what I haven't been to myself." Jorie couldn't think of anything else to say except, "I'm sorry."

"But I still don't hear why you're doing this. I know we didn't start out on a very good foot, and most of our relationship has been built during a time we really shouldn't have been building one. But that doesn't mean I love you any less. I can't imagine loving anyone more."

To Jorie it was like the day after the first time they made love, when she came to pick up her portfolio and he was so understanding. She wanted him to be an asshole, but he was so tolerant of her feelings and insightful about what she needed at that time. Right then she needed her sobriety, and there was nothing he could do to give that to her but to let her go.

As she cried harder, Bronx took her hand. "Jorie, I haven't asked you for much in the past, and I have never begged anyone for anything. But I am begging you now, please don't do this."

Throughout their entire relationship she was always his primary focus. Whatever she asked for he gave. Even when she didn't know she needed it, he was ready with the exact word, strategy or touch to fix whatever. Now he was asking her for something, for the first time, and she couldn't give it to him. Leaving him felt like her heart being blown apart, but knowing what she was doing to him felt like losing part of her soul.

Jorie knew she could sit and cry in that chair forever, but listening to him pleading with her was too much. In that moment, all the air was sucked out of the room, and she had to escape. As she rose out of the chair, she held on the hand he was grasping. "I'm so, so sorry," she whispered again, gently sliding the ring into his palm and closing his fingers over it. She was out the front door before he even knew she had done it.

Eighteen

JORIE LEANED BACK IN THE seat; her bare feet up on the dash and her hair flying around in the wind that whizzed over the top of the convertible. Her oversized sunglasses blocked the sunlight from her closed eyes. She rolled her head to the side and slowly glanced out at the dazzling blue ocean on her right, streaking by the road they were traveling on. It was an incredible blue. Jorie let out a sigh.

"You want to talk about it?" Rhea questioned.

Jorie shook her head very slowly. "I don't know. I don't know what else to say about it."

"You want to tell me how you're feeling about it? Have you talked to Bronx?"

Jorie could tell the tears were coming just hearing his name. She hadn't talked to him. They texted a couple of times so she could set up a time to come get her things. He wasn't home when she was there, and though a small part of her was wishing he would walk through the door and envelop her in his strong arms, she knew he wouldn't. Throughout their long and complicated affair, he had always respected what she'd asked of him. Jorie asked him not to be there, and he was just respecting her wishes. She loved him for that, but in a way she also hated it.

"I did," Rhea said. She looked over at Jorie, who tried her hardest not to look like somebody just held up the world's juiciest steak in front of the world's hungriest dog. "He called me the other night. I don't think he knew what else to do, or who to go to."

Jorie looked straight ahead. "What did he say?" she asked, the calm, disinterested tone she attempted really only an illusion in her mind.

"He needed to understand what happened, and he wanted to know what he could do to fix it. That man is always trying to fix everything." Jorie couldn't tell if Rhea's smile at this comment was a reflection of her esteem for Bronx or an attempt to lighten the mood. She went on. "I just said that as much as I'd love to be able to explain it, you can't really explain addiction. They can try to define it or put it in medical journals or whatever, but there's no way for him to really understand what we go through. And I said, as far as the relationship stuff, he really needed to talk to you."

"He won't," Jorie said softly. "I told him I couldn't, and I know he'll respect that until I say something different." She looked over at Rhea. "I'm just not ready."

"Then you're not ready," Rhea said matter-of-factly.

The two women drove on a bit further. Then Rhea turned to Jorie. "Did you think about what I said? About the therapy?"

Jorie grimaced. "Ohhh, I really don't want to see a shrink! I know they help some people, but I just don't think I'm ready to spill this all out to new person right now. You're all the therapist I need anyway."

"I would be, if you'd talk to me!" Rhea exclaimed. "Jorie, I'm usually a lot more hands-off with my sponsees than I am with you, but I know you left Bronx because you didn't want to start drinking again, so I don't want to see you start drinking because you left him. I can't make you go, but if you're not going to talk to me about it... I'm just saying it would be good to talk to someone."

"I know…" Jorie moaned like a teenager being lectured by her mother about poor grades. She looked back out the open side window at the ocean. The blue, blue, blue ocean.

Rhea pulled the car off at an exit, pointing at her GPS. "This is where it's saying to go," she mumbled, sounding uncertain.

The car rambled down a long, tree lined path not much wider than itself. They took the curves in the road slowly, and came out at a clearing that lead to large deserted beach. That was where the tracks ended, and Rhea was hesitant about driving in too far. She didn't know what they would do if they got her car stuck in the substantial white sand that stretched all the way to the lapping waves. She certainly didn't know anyone in Mexico to call for help, and she didn't want to risk being trapped in the middle of nowhere in a different country because her stupid car was stuck in the sand!

They parked at the top of the beach itself and both got out of the car. "How in the hell did you know about this place?" Rhea questioned.

"I've been here before," Jorie replied off-handedly. She began moving down the beach toward a make-shift dock that was positioned behind some palm trees just beyond the view from the road. Rhea followed, unsure of where they were going and what they were going to do when they got there.

Suddenly Jorie stopped walking, paused, and then turned towards Rhea. She looked like she didn't know what to say, then stammered, "I think, I umm." After another glance back at the calm water, she asserted, "I need to do this part on my own."

"OK, whatever you want sweetie," Rhea said. "I'll just be over at the car."

As usual, Jorie so appreciated Rhea's simple understanding of what she needed, what she was going through, and what *not* to say to her about it. There was never a debate, never any arguing or long discussions. When Jorie knew the right thing for her, Rhea recognized it just as sure as it was in her own head.

Once Rhea turned to walk back to the car, Jorie began to make her way through the soft sand to the small dock ahead. Her first tentative step onto the old grey planks was met with a sharp creek. Despite its frail appearance and daunting noises, Jorie could tell it was as solid as the day she had stepped onto it as a child, years earlier.

So many flashes flooded into Jorie's brain, she couldn't keep them all straight. She saw herself, a little girl so intimidated by the vast expanse of water that stretched out forever from the dock. She could almost feel a breeze blow by her, remembering Addie running fearlessly down the boards and jumping into the sparkling water. Jorie had watched her in amazement, fear giving way to envy. Her sister could always do that to her; always the embodiment of what Jorie wanted to be, doing what Jorie couldn't or wouldn't. She loved Addie, and she couldn't help but yearn for that kind of confidence.

"Come on Jor, get in!" Addie yelled. "The water is really warm."

The twinkle of light off the gently rolling waves moved Jorie's thought pattern ahead to a balmy afternoon with Bronx at the resort where they had taken their vacation together. She could see him diving into a large rolling wave, his muscular back working like a sharp knife to lacerate the water before it filled in, swallowing up his whole body.

Jorie cautiously continued walking to the end of the dock. She wasn't concerned about the structure's stability. She was concerned about her own. At the last plank, Jorie stopped, set down the box she carried in her hand, and sat down slowly. Her feet dangled in the warm water, and in her mind played the laughing and splashing of children in what was now calm, still water up to her ankles.

Lacing her fingers behind her neck, Jorie tilted her head up to the vacant blue sky. Though her dark glasses already blocked most of the sunlight, she still saw a brilliant yellow light as she closed her eyes. Imprints of the sun, as well as the imprints of her past that refused to leave her head now.

She started by praying the 9th Step prayer in her head, something she had done before every amends she had made in her program. This time was different though. It wasn't about what she had done to someone else. It wasn't about facing another person whom she had harmed. This time the patience, tolerance, love and forgiveness she was praying for was directed at her. This time was much harder.

The box that lay next to her on the dock seemed to be screaming at her, and though she was suddenly hesitant to open it, she gingerly lifted the cover and put it to the side. Her hands trembling, she took out the item on top. It was a picture of her, taken the night before her surgery. She had dreaded taking it at the time, and cringed every time she looked at it since, but was now glad she had it. It reminded her of where she had been, and how far she had come. Despite the failings she had endured in her personal life since having bariatric surgery, Jorie still believed it was one of the best things she had ever done for herself. Never in her adult life had she felt so free of the grip food had over her life. That was also due to her participation in OA, but that was more about her mental state. The physical limitations that her surgery provided allowed her to put down the damn fork long enough to realize what a mess she had made of her body by overeating. Maybe she could have or should have done it the "natural" way, as people who lost weight with traditional dietary restrictions and exercise sometimes put it. Jorie knew there was nothing unnatural about her surgery, and had learned to let those remarks roll off her back. As for how she shed the pounds, there was no doubt in her mind that she had made the right decision for herself and her health. And because of that, no matter the mistakes she had made along the way, there was no way she would ever want to go back to being that woman in the picture.

Jorie took a final look at the picture and said quietly, "The way I treated you, with eating like I did, not exercising, not taking care of myself. There is no excuse for it. But it will never happen again, and I will do everything I can to never let myself ever get that unhealthy." It felt funny to be saying it out loud, but she had discussed it with Rhea and decided if she was really going to make amends to herself, it had to be like she had done with everybody else. She had to say it, weird as it felt, to know in her heart that she meant it. So she did.

She ripped the picture into as tiny of pieces as it would let her, and tossed it into the water. Just as she let it go, a very slight breeze blew up from the otherwise motionless air, and carried the pieces just a little farther out into the ocean.

The next item in her box was a cork. Jorie hadn't been in any shape to keep her head on straight, let alone the cork from the last bottle of wine she had on the way to the rehab center that frightening night over a year earlier. But Bronx kept it, and had given it to her in Mexico when they celebrated her six months of sobriety. He told her the story of how his father kept the cap from the last bottle of beer he drank before getting sober. At the time, Jorie felt a little uncomfortable carrying it, hell even holding it. It was like paraphernalia. But she held on to it, trusting Bronx and his ability to always provide her with what she needed exactly when she needed it. He had been right then, and remembering the night he gave it to her made Jorie want to burst into tears, find the nearest phone and call him that instant. She forced herself back into the moment instead, praying for guidance once again, to focus on the task at hand and remember why she was there.

"Every drink," she began softly, "that I took that lead me into the disease of alcoholism felt like a step into the darkest pits of hell, and at the same time the only thing on this earth that could save me from it. My affair with Bronx was a drug, just like the booze. They were the wrong things to use to deal with the problems in my life, and I will do everything in my power, with God's constant help and support, to make sure I never go down that road again."

Jorie had forgiven herself in Step 4, something that seemed backwards to her at the time. Of course she could forgive others for what they'd done to her, and still make amends for what she did to them five steps later. But how could she forgive herself for something she hadn't apologized for yet? As she kicked her feet back and forth in the warm water, it became clear to her. Without having cleared out the anger and resentment towards herself earlier in her program, Jorie would have never been able to say those things to herself in her amends. It would have been a hurried 'I'm sorry,' or an empty promise to never do it again. Because she gave herself permission to be loving and kind without all the baggage, it made the work of both making amends and forgiving herself so much easier.

As she had the picture, Jorie tossed the cork out into the serene waters. It hit and bobbed there like, well, like a cork. The image tied to the phrase made Jorie chuckle out loud. She leaned back on her arms, the heat from the sun warming her whole body. Slowly her eyes closed, and she proceeded with more of her amends. Jorie knew she couldn't possibly make up for all the wrongs she had done herself in life. She was so grateful to Rhea in that moment, for having shown her that it's not necessary to say you're sorry for every little thing, and that she had to let go of so many of the things that were just the result of human nature. It was the big things, the actions that had led Jorie to the darkest places in her life that needed to be corrected. Those were the ones that she was there to deal with. She wasn't going to sweat the small stuff. It all fit in somewhere in the overall scheme of her life's misdeeds. Jorie understood that if she could make amends for the big ones, the little ones would all be covered as well.

Nineteen

FINALLY, SHE SAT BACK UP straight, and reached into the box for the only item left. It was the key to the house in which Jorie had grown up. She had carried that key with her for years, using it to let herself in after school, after dates, on weekends home from college. It was the way into the safety and sometimes insanity of her family. It had saved her life once, and for that she had never been able to forgive herself.

Near the end of her junior year in college, Jorie was rushed one Friday evening getting home from class. She dropped her bag on the kitchen table of her tiny apartment, changed into the only dress she owned, and ran back out the door. Though she knew her sister would understand Jorie being late, as she usually was, this was one time she really wanted to be on time. Partly out of respect for her sister, and partly because Jorie knew she was one of the few people who could keep civility when her parents were both in the room together. She really needed to be there, not just on time but maybe even early.

Jorie's stomach started to turn as she put her car in gear and tore out of the apartment parking lot. As she headed down the street in the direction of her old neighborhood, Jorie grabbed her cell phone, flipped it open and hit two on the speed dial for Addie's number. Her sister answered on the first ring.

"Jor, where are you? Dad and Ellen just got here, and I can tell it's already making mom crazy!" Addie sounded as frantic as Jorie felt, but she didn't want to feed into her older sister's mood. What Addie needed was somebody calm. Jorie could be that person in her family any time she had to, which was pretty often.

"I'm coming, I'm coming. I'm on my way. Just…keep mom and dad at opposite ends of the table. Maybe he can bore Jason with some old high school sports stories. It will be fine." Jorie kept her tone even and low. Maybe freshman psych wasn't such a waste of tuition money after all.

Addie seemed to calm down a bit, but Jorie expected her sister would be on edge all the way until the wedding. It was the night of their engagement party. Addie's fiancé, Jason, was from out of state, and his parents were even flying in for the weekend. Jason's sister was going to pick them up at the airport, and they would all be there in time for the big party following the family dinner that Addie had wanted, with Jorie and their parents at the restaurant where Addie and Jason had gone on their first date. She was very sentimental like that, and though it usually drove Jorie crazy, in this case she found it kind of cute.

"Shit!" Addie exclaimed, and Jorie rolled her eyes. Well that eye of the storm was short lived. "Jorie, you have to go by mom's house for me. There's a box on the counter, a jewelry box. It has this tie clip in it of grandpa's that mom had redone so I could give it to Jason tonight. I really need to have it. Pleeease! You have to bring it!"

"Addie, I don't even have my key for the house. It's hanging in my apartment," Jorie began, though she put her signal on and pulled into the left turn lane to make a u-turn. She knew it was pointless to argue with her sister when she was like this.

Addie's tone changed from the earlier hysteria. "It's OK, you can be late. I will handle things here. Just please go get your key and then go by mom's and get me the tie clip. I *have* to have it tonight. Please!"

Jorie shook her head, rolled her eyes again (though nobody was around to see the gestures) and assured her sister that her precious tie clip would indeed be at that restaurant that night. Even though it meant Jorie would have to go back to her apartment, get the key, then drive to their mother's house and get the clip, and then finally drive to dinner. Sure, no problem. That's what Jorie was usually there for.

After a dozen or so thank you's, the two sisters said I love you and hung up the phone. It was the last time Jorie talked to Addie, or anyone else in her family.

By the time she had finally reached the restaurant, Jorie was being passed by fire trucks with screaming sirens and ambulances with blinding red lights. At first she was mildly annoyed by this, as she was already running so late. But the closer she got to the short driveway up to the restaurant, the faster her heart began to race. It seemed they were all going to the same place she was. Goosebumps broke out all over her skin, and her head began to spin.

She couldn't get anywhere near the building, so she parked as close as she could and began running through the crowd, pushing her way through the onlookers who had gathered in a large hoard. It was hard to get through, but she finally managed to make it to a cutoff point where the firemen were blocking people from the scene.

"M'am, I'm sorry, but you can't come any closer," a burley looking fireman explained, putting up his hand and keeping Jorie back with the crowd.

"But my family was in there!" she practically screamed. Partly because of adrenaline, partly because the trucks, water, fire, and crowd combined into a deafening noise that made it hard to hear anything. "Where are the people who were in the restaurant?" she demanded.

The fireman looked over his shoulder at a small group of people near a decorative park bench and trees that lined the side of the establishment. Some of them were obviously employees, donning their white shirts and black pants under the stiff green blankets the police and EMT's had wrapped around their shoulders. They looked wet. The sprinklers, Jorie thought. They must have gotten wet from the sprinkler system.

As the fireman looked back at Jorie, she almost became hysterical. The look on his face, combined with the absence of her family in the crowd of restaurant employees and other diners who were all congregated in one place, made her body tremble from the inside out. She refused to believe it could be as bad as she was imagining.

"I can check for you, but you really have to stay back. It's too dangerous to get any closer. Some people have been transported to the hospital. Give me the names of your family members and I'll see what I can find out." The fireman seemed sincere enough, but Jorie was concerned by the look on his face. It was grey and hollow, and the words he offered seemed to be some sort of stall tactic. She could feel her chest getting tighter.

Scanning the area as quickly as she could, Jorie couldn't seem to find anybody from her family in any of the groups she could see. The sky had grown dark early, and the only light now was that from the fire, and the revolving red from the fire trucks. The color blinked over and over on the faces in the crowd, but none of them belonged to Addie, her parents, step mother or a soon-to-be brother-in-law.

The fireman returned much faster than she had expected. Jorie looked at him with the most hopeful expression ever. He refused to meet her eyes, and instead instructed her to follow him to a waiting patrol car near the edge of the fire scene. She sat in the backseat, door open; waiting for the officer she was told would be right over to talk to her. Grateful they'd given her a place to sit down before her legs gave out, Jorie waited endlessly for the police officer to come speak with her. In reality, it was only a couple of minutes, but to Jorie, at that moment, it felt like every minute that had ever passed in the history of the world.

"Jorie Jones?" the female officer asked quietly as she approached the car. For a second Jorie felt a bit of relief. How would they know her name, unless her family was out safe and had told somebody there to keep an eye out for her when she arrived. It was a good sign, but her respite from the terror of the past few minutes was brief. When Officer Clarc (Jorie knew she would never forget her name) slowly lowered herself down to eye level with Jorie, everything went completely blank. Even though it happened more than 15 years earlier, she still could not remember the rest of the events of that night, or much of the next few days.

Later she was told by family and friends what had happened. They were the only memories she had of those hours and days following, and she knew they weren't based on her actual recollection of what happened. It was the difference between reading what happens in a movie scene on paper, and actually seeing the movie. There's no doubt where that visual image comes from, and Jorie's recall was all just 2-dimensional descriptions of what happened.

Officer Clarc informed Jorie that her stepmother, Ellen, was en route to the hospital with very severe burns. She was not expected to recover, but had been found alive and was being treated as best they could. Her whole family had been in a private room in the back of the building. Jorie knew that sounded right; Addie had talked of nothing else but reserving that room for their engagement party since the day she gotten her diamond ring. It was too small for the wedding reception itself, but it meant the world to her to celebrate her life with Jason in the place where they had first dated and fallen in love.

"Jorie," Officer Clarc suddenly said more intently, "the fire fighters are doing all they can to get this put out. Everyone we know of who is out is accounted for. Right now, we don't have anyone from your family but Ellen, and she was able to tell us where everybody else is in the building. And to look for you. So I need you to hang on with me for just a little bit here. I'm going to check with the fire chief and see what is happening. Can you be alright here for a couple of minutes?"

It took Jorie an extra 22 minutes to return to her apartment for the key to her mother's house. Twenty-two minutes earlier she would have arrived at the restaurant and been sitting with her family when the gas line that exploded in the kitchen took out the entire back half of the building, along with Jorie's family and eight other people that night. Her step-mother Ellen, who had been in the restroom at the time, was able to be rescued through a back window, but succumbed to her injuries the next morning. According to the fire investigator's report, which Jorie had read over and over until she memorized it, the first call about the explosion came in to 9-1-1 nineteen minutes after hanging up from her call with Addie. The way she figured it, that would have given her six final minutes of time with her parents and sister before the end came for all of them. But Jorie wasn't there. She had to go home to get her key.

Turning the key over and over in her palm, as she had done so many times before, Jorie looked at the dull brassy color and the three cut-outs near the top that she always used to recognize what exactly it opened. "You saved my life that night," she practically whispered. "But now it's time to save my own life. I know I couldn't have done anything differently, and I know I'm supposed to still be here on this earth. I have three beautiful children to prove that. I can't be accountable for what happened anymore, and I can't hold you accountable for what didn't." And with that, Jorie tossed the key as far as she could muster. It went much further than the photograph or the cork, and landed with an unremarkable plunk in the silky blue waters of the endless ocean.

Jorie's feet dragged through the light pale sand which sifted under her toes and into her flip flops. As she slowly made her way back to the car, Rhea stood up from where she was leaning on the hood.

"Done?" Rhea asked simply.

Jorie nodded, wrapped her arms around her friend as tears slowly ran down her cheeks. There was nothing that could be said. Rhea embraced her for a moment, and then grabbed her gently by the arms.

"Are you ready?"

"Yeah," Jorie said, taking in a deep breath and smiling. Her smile was genuine, and the air she exhaled seemed to push out all the demons she had been ceaselessly fighting. As she walked around to the passenger door, Jorie turned and looked one more time at the tranquil blue of the ocean. She slowly closed her eyes, then opened them again. Finally, she could breathe.